Wings and Wolf's Bane

Scent of an Angel, Volume 1

Susan Stec and Christopher James Rizzo

Published by Susan Stec, 2023.

WINGS AND WOLF'S BANE

First edition. December 14, 2023.

Copyright © 2023 Susan Stec and Christopher James Rizzo.

ISBN: 979-8223724100

Written by Susan Stec and Christopher James Rizzo.

Table of Contents

Scent of an Angel

WINGS AND WOLF'S BANE
BOOK ONE

Susan Stec & Christopher James Rizzo

First Edition, June 2020
Cover Design by Susan Stec
Edited by Genevieve Scholl
Formatted by Genevieve Scholl

Chapter One

R EKA
I bit my lip hard, mouth salivating at the taste of copper. My bones stretched and popped while sweat dampened my lower back. The wolf in me strained to be free. I gripped the wooden swing under us, my feet planted firmly on the back porch of our home.

"We owe it to the pack, Reka," Peter said. "With ten males and only three females, it's all about survival. And you're the only she-wolf without a mate. If you wait until you turn eighteen, your father has the right to choose for you. You know I don't want that. Do you?"

Not like I haven't heard this before. Only a million, zillion, freaking times a week from just about every wolf in the pack.

"At least you get to choose," Peter said. "I mean, being the Alpha's daughter has its good points."

It had no good points. I ran my hand over the pocket of my jeans and the razor blade resting against my leg.

"If you pick me," Peter said through a smile. "You know I have your back. I would never hold you to anything that your father or the pack expects of us. "

I studied Peter's face. No doubt I was attracted to him, and there was fire if I let it surface. But Dad wanted this.

Peter was a month older than me, black hair, sky-blue eyes, and a wicked alpha smile. His wolf side was scary threatening. Last Saturday I watched him kick butt at the challenge practice session. There are good fighters in the pack and there are better fighters. Peter is better. That didn't encourage me to pick him, especially if I was forced. If I wanted that kind of life, Peter would be my wolf. But I didn't.

Male alphas were always challenging each other. It's kind of a pain. But I loved to watch. I longed to be part of the training sessions. But that was a male only role.

Peter was the youngest male in our pack, everyone else available is too old. Actually, David was twenty-five but an omega, mild-mannered, easy going, loyal, definitely not a fighter. He did the pack books, paid bills, cleaned house, and even cooked occasionally. Although David would be less maintenance than Peter, there was no fire. Those were my only choices as far as Dad was concerned, *if* I wanted to stay in the pack.

Jade is another option. There's definitely fire there. Crap!

Jade was a fae that lived Down Under, a gaming buddy. There was definitely an attraction on both our parts, but I'd have to leave the pack. My mother had been fae. I never met her. She died giving birth to me and my sister. I haven't explored that side of me, and hardly ever talked about it around the pack, another thing my father forbid.

I promised Peter I would never go Down Under without him, and told myself pack life, and my ability to be and alpha was a bigger draw than asserting my fae side.

I could always go to one of the other packs. There were five: Big Rapids, Cadillac, White Cloud, Tustin, and us, Reed City. But the whole point was, I didn't want a mate. What good was having a choice if there was really no choice at all? Not now and probably not ever. I hated it.

"You don't have to love me."

Peter's words dragged my attention to his plea, but I didn't look at him.

"No demands. No promises," he said.

Statements like that irked me. As an alpha she-wolf, I should have the choice to be an active part of the pack's safety and welfare with or without a mate after I turn eighteen, not just respected for having children. Dad argues that being pregnant offered a she-wolf lots of protection in our pack, as well as other packs in our territory. It was like the only thing that kept peace in the tri-county packs. 'With growth comes strength,' Dad always said. 'Being female is a gift to the whole pack, Reka.' *Yeah. Right. Everyone except me.*

The porch swing was hard under my butt. I pressed my knuckles on the front pocket of my jeans. A razor rested there, and through the fabric it pinched my skin. I encouraged it over and over again. I had control over that pain. And I knew if *I wanted to* I could draw blood.

The sun hung low in front of me. It lit a trail of fall color down the dirt path out of here and onto the two-lane blacktop on the other side of one hundred acres of woods. I flared my nostrils and inhaled; the moon clawed at my back, called to me. In another hour, the packs would be immersed in bloodlust, and the first night of a full-moon hunt.

"...and if you do choose me, we don't have to mate right away," Peter was saying. "Hell, I can wait until you're ready. You just need to accept the bond until we become of age. And then if you still feel the same way this time next year, I promise, I'll release you."

He'll release me. He'll let me. He'll wait. Him, him, him.

He looked at me, blue eyes carrying sadness and deep longing. I knew he was trying to help. I also knew he loved me.

I loved him, too. I really did. He was the best friend I ever had. The only friend, actually, if you didn't count a couple of the older pack members.

"If you don't let me bite you, someone else will," he said again.

Ugh! I hate when he makes sense. Especially when I'm not ready to accept it!

"Are you done?" I asked and ran my tongue over the place where I'd bit the inside of my lower lip a few minutes ago. The coppery taste was distant, but the smell of the blood under the razor was strong.

"Look," I said, "I want out of this. I'm sick of being someone's property. Today it's my father, tomorrow it would be a mate. Constant monitoring, guards; my father's demands are making me crazy. Crap, I hate him, Peter, and I don't want to hate you too. You know what I'm capable of. I have no doubt I could take down most of the males in our pack. But I'm not allowed to try. It sucks. I wish we could trade places for just a month. Then maybe you'd be more sympathetic."

Peter put his head down, pushed air out his nose, and watched his feet do nothing below the swing.

I shoved my hand into my pocked, gripped the razor and gritted my teeth. Peter may be the hunkiest guy in the pack, and if I were a submissive, we would have probably been good, but I never met a guy willing to give it up to a girl, especially an alpha male.

I shook my head. "Two strong-willed leaders in the same cage? Nope. It isn't going to work."

"So, are you saying you're going to choose David over me?"

Now he looked angry.

"You just don't get it!" I said and tipped the razor on end. I felt the corner poke through the material and prick my thigh.

"What?" Peter shouted. "How about you tell me what I don't get?"

Before I said something I'd totally regret, I stiffened my lips and caught a breath with a sharp pain on my thigh.

"I didn't think so," he said. "Because you don't get it either."

This was useless. I was already second in command, just by being my father's daughter. After I turned eighteen in a few weeks, should my father fall ill or go missing, I would be temporally in charge of the pack. But the catch was I couldn't fight for my right to keep leadership. Only males could challenge each other for the win. I'd die before stepping back and my father knew that. That was why he encouraged me to pick Peter, an alpha who would automatically take my place as second.

There is always Jade.

I wanted to scream. Instead, I locked eyes with Peter. Wolf sense nudged me: Peter was smart. He'd make a good mate. Our children would be a force to reckon with. I felt rage run from the pit of my stomach to the back of my throat. Hell, Jade would probably expect the same.

"Why can't I fight on Saturday, Peter? Why can't I try out for leadership? Why don't I bite you, mark you, and you can be my property? Huh? To my dad, women are mothers first, and anything that comes after that is not a priority. You are an alpha male. You don't get it?"

"I do get it," Peter said.

Crap.

"Look, let's back away from this right nowt," Peter said with minimal anger, but tons angst. "I'll stay close when we hunt tonight. Fair enough?""

"No one owns me, Peter." I blinked at the threat of tears. "Not my father. Not the pack. And not even you."

His eyes moved to the pocket of my jeans where my fingers gripped the razor.

"Right now, I want to hunt," I said before we were both crying. "By myself, so if—"

"You need to stop cutting yourself," he whispered.

Blood seeped through the material where I had pushed the point of the razor with frustration.

Peter's caring eyes and hurt expression cranked adrenaline, made me want to hunt even more. Another thirty minutes and neither of us would be able to stop the change anyway. I felt the moon struggle to rise as I tried to ignore the pull.

"I should be able to hunt without a guard. This isn't fair, and you know it. Maybe it was fifty years ago, but not today."

"Maybe it is time for change. Women should have the right to choose," he said, "but there are things that will never change. We will always have to fight for our territory, choose who hunts our woods, and the freedom to make laws within our pack. There's strength and power in numbers, and you can't deny that. That's why women have always been treated differently."

"Oh, come on. You're really going there? No one tries to take what isn't theirs anymore."

Peter shook his head. "You're wrong. The Big Rapids pack has twenty members, and seven are women. Out of the seven, four are unmarked and coming of age this year. We only have you because your sister is not an option. She is not a shifter. Your father won't let her take the chance because it could kill her." He tightened his lips "If we don't grow...well, it's wolf nature to overtake and rule. It won't be long before Big Rapids makes a stand."

Double Crap! He might be right. The Big Rapids alpha was already making demands. They asked to join our hunt tonight. And Dad wasn't majorly happy about letting it happen.

"Maybe you should just let me mark you so no one else can."

"No. This is a matter of principal. I should have the right to be part of the pack in any capacity I can back up."

Looking up at the sky, Peter softly growled. "Damn that alpha strength!"

The smile on his face made me hide a grin.

Peter started to speak but a rabbit darted across the path thirty feet away. I jumped off the porch swing. The pad of my right foot lightly touched the porch rail and I leapt. With sharp pains, that I embraced, I felt bones crack, pop, and elongate. When I landed on the cool grass, I was a wolf, pulse accelerated, nose to the trail.

Being the only pack member who could phase to wolf on the run was a gift not many werewolves had. If I were male, I would be at the front of the pack defending and protecting.

I opened my maw and blew a howl. Peter shouted for me to wait. I heard his bones crack. It would take him minutes to complete the change. And by then, like me, he would have lost interest in the argument.

On the run, a scent of the rabbit's fear drove me. My legs kicked up dirt and the hair on my belly scraped tall grass. As always, I wondered where my clothes went and dismissed the thought because I was always the black-haired, green-eyed, human with purple streaks in her hair and clothes on.

The sun through the trees electrified the woods with fall color. The smell of small furry animals made my mouth water. The razor cuts on my thighs tightened under my fur and tingled. They were healing rapidly. I stopped short, skidded, rolled sideways, and wrapped my teeth around the itch on my right thigh. Lips back, gums protruded, my teeth nibbled incessantly at the healing cuts. Man, it felt good to be in fur again.

Out of the corner of my eye, the rabbit zigzagged across the path. Razor cuts had healed and were forgotten. I ran with excitement coursing through the veins of a lean, agile predator. The thrill of a kill pushed me through the tall grass at the edge of the path and down the hill into the woods.

For the most part, the leaves were still holding on to branches and the ones that had given up were supple under my paws. Eyes on the prize, moving stealthily, low to the ground, I teased my dinner. The rabbit scrambled through the underbrush and I lost sight of it. But its scent was heavy. I paused, and snorted—the wolf equivalent of a snicker—then took off. The dirt smelled rich and damp from a late afternoon rain. My muscles stretched and tightened as I hurtled fallen tree limbs and darted under or over brush.

The crisp air felt good as I pulled it in and pushed it out of my lungs. When I caught sight of the rabbit again, it was inches away. I pounced to the right, and it sidled left circling birch trees and nettle. Careful not to get scratched, I jumped fallen branches like hurtles at our high school track events. The rabbit glanced back through a cluster of birch and seemed to realize it had run out of prickly bush to slow me down. I caught a scent of animal urine and knew it had been a passing doe, and then smelled the rabbit's burrow. It was close. She skidded toward it sideways and scampered under several dried-out branches on the ground. I was on her before she went ten feet. One swift bite and a shake of my head and her neck snapped; she lay limp in my mouth. I placed her on the ground in front of me and licked blood from my maw. Holding the animal with my paw, I nosed her head to the side, got a good grip on the fur covered skin beneath her neck, and ripped. The meat underneath was still warm.

I looked down at what was left of my prize. A small pile of fur. Thoughts of the weekend ahead of me backed bloody bile up my throat. My stomach heaved, and my body began to change. I hated when that happened directly after a kill.

Like all the other wolves, I had a connection to my pack and felt my father's anger at my starting without them on the first night of a moon-hunt. Especially since Big Rapids pack might be joining us. That made me smile as I slipped into the comforting shadows of the woods.

Chapter Two

CALASTAIR

A flash of light, a clap of thunder, and I found myself standing in a cluttered room. Earth was the farthest I'd ever traveled before and the effects of the teleport left me woozy. I fell to one knee as my eyes spun in their sockets. It took a few minutes before I was able to lift my head to take in my new surroundings. Posters of bands featuring men with long hair and dark clothing were scattered across the wall, and a collage of clothes splayed underfoot. It was dark, musky, and unpleasant. Everything I knew it would be.

The argument I just had with my dad still thundered in my ear. Phrases like *There are certain ways angels should act,* and *you have too much of your mother in you* echoed longer than the others. I remember the look in his eye when he said the Angels were banishing me to Earth till I could learn to behave more 'respectfully'.

Before I was able to take in all my surroundings, there were three sharp knocks on the door. A middle-aged woman with curly brown hair and a baby tucked in her right arm barged in.

"Calastair. Good," she said. "I thought I heard you arrive."

I winced at hearing my full name. "It's Cal, and who are you?"

"Okay. Cal then. I'm Lana, your caretaker, dear," she said sweetly and upbeat. "I'll be looking after you while you're on Earth."

I gritted my teeth; this must have been my father's idea. "I'm three hundred and fifty years old; I don't need a babysitter."

"You're three hundred and fifty in angel years. In human years, that's about seventeen," she explained. "And seventeen-year-olds on Earth need to have a legal guardian. That's me." Before I could respond, she waved me into the hallway. "Come along; mornings are very busy in this house. I look after many wayward children here that wouldn't quite ... fit in a normal house."

I sighed as she disappeared around the corner. I hated being ordered around, but if I were to be allowed back in heaven, I'd have to play along. With hunched shoulders and an indignant expression, I followed along.

We hurried down a narrow hall with green and blue shag carpeting. Its musty smell hung in the heavy air. Sounds of children in the other rooms echoed off the bare walls.

Lana wore a bland yellow dress with white flowers. It took me a second to see she had a brown furry tail poking out the back of it. I was going to ask about it when two small kids with bright red hair pushed past us. Halfway down the hallway, they disappeared in a portal made of fire.

"Holy shit! What are they?!" I asked, startled.

"Oh, don't worry about them. Also, do you think your father would approve of that language?" she asked scornfully.

"My dad, the angel? Heh. No way." A smile slid across my face. "But my Mom was a Fae; I'm sure she wouldn't have minded."

The woman shook her head. "Yes, yes, I'm familiar with your lineage. Very impressive," she said plainly. "Let's just keep the swearing to a minimum in my house if you would please. That's the reason you were cast out of heaven you know."

"Because of my swearing?" I laughed.

"No, because of your Mom's rebellious spirit. There were some angels a long time ago that were rebellious... it did not end well," she said, disappearing down the stairwell.

I scampered after her, being careful not to catch my toes on the ridiculous thick carpet. "Is that what this is about? I did some harmless pranks, that's all. It hardly makes me the next Lucifer, does it?"

"That's not my department, dear. I'm just the caretaker."

We walked into the house's kitchen. A small table sat in the middle with at least a dozen kids around it. Most were under ten years old; I was definitely the oldest in the house. The room blared with children's laughter, screams, and gobbling food noises. I had thought the house couldn't get any uglier, but the flower wallpaper lining the kitchen proved me wrong.

Lana plopped the baby in a highchair at the end of the table. She looked at me with a warm smile. "Would you like any cereal? I got all kinds."

"No."

"How about some toast, or an English muffin?"

"Angels don't need food," I said, trying to sound polite.

"You may not have needed it in heaven, but you'll need to eat here." She shoved her arms into the pantry and quickly dug through a sea of boxes. "At least take a granola bar in case you change your mind," she said, presenting me with a rectangular wrapper.

"Oh, uh...thanks." I slipped the bar into my jean pocket. The thought of actually chewing and swallowing dead plants and animals was still disgusting to me. "Look, what I really want is to know what I need to do to be allowed back home. My dad said something about a trial I'd have to do. Any idea what that is?"

Lana grabbed a glass one of the kids tried to knock over. "Sure, hold on." She hurried over to a table and started sorting through papers. She pulled out an envelope lined with gold and handed it to me. "Here's what they gave me. They said if you do a good job, they'll let you back in heaven. If not ... well, your dad wasn't completely clear on that."

"Whatever," I said, taking the envelope. I tore it open and pulled out a piece of paper. On it was one word, written in silver ink.

Reka

"What is this?" I asked, holding up the letter.

"Your trial, dear."

"But it's just a name," I said, aggravated. "What exactly am I supposed to do?"

Lana shrugged, her attention split between me and keeping the kids from destroying the kitchen. "That's not my department either. I'd guess you're supposed to help her in some way."

"No way," I said. "Guardian Angel duty?" I threw my head back and closed my eyes "Laaaame."

"Not exactly the best attitude to take."

"Doesn't mean it's not true." I turned the paper over to make sure there wasn't anything on the back. There was not. "Just how am I supposed to find this person?"

Lana chased after a piece of toast that had been thrown across the room. "Reed City is a small town, Cal; I'm sure it won't be too hard for you to figure out."

My jaw clenched. I didn't know what to expect during this trial, but I had assumed it was something more exciting than this. Worse yet, there were no instructions on the letter, so to find out how to help this Reka, I'd have to talk to her. And the idea of talking to one of these lower life forms was so … demeaning. "Fine. How hard could it be? I'll just find her, figure out what her deal is, and then get off this primitive plain of existence." I snapped my fingers in an attempt to teleport. But nothing happened.

The action finally drew the attention of all the children at the table. They looked at me with curiosity. One of them, a young blonde girl, stuck her purple forked tongue at me and laughed.

"Oh yeah, the angels also wanted me to let you know your powers have been limited for this trial," Lana chimed. "And by limited, I mean you're basically a human; things like teleporting, flying, and other more obvious abilities aren't available."

"What?! How is that fair?!"

"There's a saying here, 'life isn't fair.' The angels were afraid you wouldn't show the proper restraint and do something to expose what you are."

Those words sounded exactly like something my dad would say. He always assumed I'd screw up everything I touched. Well, fine, if that was how he wanted to play it, I'd do this without powers. If for no reason than to show him he was wrong.

"I guess I'll just put one foot in front of the other like all insignificant mammals here," I growled, and walked out of the kitchen.

"Your class schedule is on the table by the door. Dinner is at six tonight," Lana's voice chased after me. "At least be home before dark."

But this rundown house wasn't my home. And all I wanted to do was return to my real one.

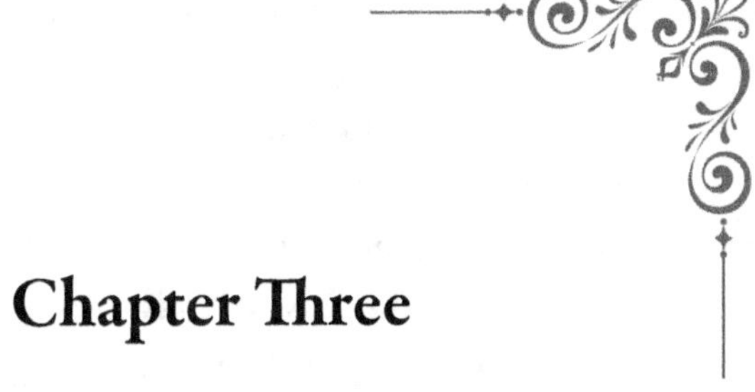

Chapter Three

R^{EKA} "I am really not looking forward to breakfast, Buddy," I
stroked his silky brindle ears. He looked up at me with large brown
eyes full of innocence. But small Caviler was stubborn as a mule.
Neither of us liked being told what to do.

Buddy wagged his tail and jumped down from the rumpled
camouflage comforter on my bed. He sat beside me, tongue lolling.
I smiled down at him. "Yep, it's a school day. I don't like that
either—hate mixing with humans, especially ones my age. They
have their priorities all screwed up."

Buddy was the only furry animal in the house that I could say
anything at all to without worrying about it later. Even with Peter,
I held some things closer to my chest. The rest of the family just
didn't get me at all. But Buddy did.

In my underwear, I turned a circle in front of a full-length
mirror. My breasts were too big. My butt too small. And at
four-feet-eleven inches, I was too short for most guys my age. But
I had a killer waist; only twenty inches. Unfortunately, it got lost
between Mount Vesuvius and the wastelands of my buttocks.
When you wear a size one bathing suit bottom, and a size twelve
top, it's hard to find clothes that look great on you. I hated my

boobs. At least, when I was the Wolf, I didn't have them to deal with.

It was not like I wanted to look sexy or cute, or anything special. In fact, I really didn't want to be visible at all. I didn't try to keep up with popularity among anyone my age, and Peter and I stuck together. We didn't have friends. Eleventh grade girls were all about looks and dating guys. Why couldn't I just have guy friends? Guys were much more fun to hang out with than to kiss.

Buddy nose-tapped my ankle and whined. I pulled my eyes off my image and reached down and patted his head. He raised his butt and I scratched his back down to his wagging tail.

"Girls like to gossip, Buddy. They're always trying to one-up each other, and they cover up natural scents with lavender, rose, or musk. I bet that would annoy you, too, right?" I wrinkled my nose and snorted.

Buddy snorted and pushed a little bark of agreement.

"Can you believe all of them crush on newest buzzes on the top ten—and they call it music—completely ignoring Mother Earth's music?"

I bet they never sat in the woods and listened to a bird's song, or squirrel chatter, a coyote's howl, or the rustle of fall leaves.

Buddy eagerly awaited my next words. I wiggled my nose. "No sweat, little guy. A few more months and I am so out of there." I picked him up, tucked him under my arm, and nose-bump-kissed him. His feet wiggled and tickled my arms.

I set Buddy on the wooden floor and stomped over to my bed. The kitchen was just below me, and Dad probably sat at the table waiting for me to come down so he could tell me everywhere I was lacking. I exhaled through my mouth, picked up one of Buddy's toys, and tossed it into my open closet. He scampered over and started rummaging through my shoes.

My baggiest jeans laid on my bed—the ones with the holes in the knees and butt—and I pulled them on. A small section of the left front pocket hung out of a hole in the jeans and I tucked it back in.

Dad hated the jeans.

I pulled a red T-shirt, two sizes too big, off the bed and dragged it over my head. The T-shirt read; **Will you just stop talking**.

Dad hated the shirt, too.

I snagged my hairbrush from the dresser, leaned over, and brushed purple streaks toward the floor. Dad hated the Raz color streaks, too. I didn't get all the drama. It was my body, my hair.

Buddy boogied out of the closet and ran for my swaying hair. I laughed, set the hairbrush on the floor, shook my fingers through my hair, and flipped my head up before he got a mouthful. Buddy scampered under the bed with the hairbrush.

"You better not chew that up, Buddy," I teased. And he would if I didn't wrestle it from him.

I looked at myself in the mirror and thought, *you look great*. But really, I didn't. And I was okay with that. I slipped bare feet into black, ankle-high *All Star's* and jogged downstairs to the kitchen.

My twin sister, a human—lucky her—was at the stove in front of pans full of sizzling bacon and eggs. Zrinka didn't look at all like me. She favored our mother; fair skinned, dark blonde hair, brown eyes, delicate frame, long legs, small breasts, small waist, curvy hips, and a perfect butt. The only thing Zrinka and I shared from Mom was her slight of height.

I smelled biscuits in the oven and my mouth watered. But then Dad turned the same angry black eyes on me that I often used on him. Zrinka was fair like Mom. I had dark features like dad.

Buddy moved from me to Zrinka, hopping up and down on short little legs. My sister tossed him a small piece of bacon, and it went straight to his tummy.

I pulled my glare off my father and laughed at Buddy. "Did you even taste that?" I asked the pup and bent over to try to snag him. He took off in the direction of the food source.

"How did you get out of your cage last night, you little stinker?" Zrinka asked Buddy but continued with a tease for me. "I woke and he was asleep on my other pillow."

My sister laughed as she dumped some scrambled eggs on the dish in front of my chair. She knew I didn't like Buddy in her room. She also knew I only put the dog in his cage if he was in danger.

"Good morning, Reka," Dad said, and pulled my attention back to him. "I assume you had a good hunt last night. I didn't see or hear you. Did you even go out?"

"Yes," I said, but Dad knew that. The call of a full moon was impossible to resist, especially for a shifter under eighteen. "Look, if this is going to be one of those mornings where I wake up in a good mood after a great hunt, and you burst the first bubble of bliss I've experienced in weeks, I'm out of here."

Zrinka gave Buddy another piece of bacon and glared at me. "Could you at least wait until after breakfast before you become the bitch you usually are when you wake?"

We were not allowed to cuss in the house, but a bitch is a female wolf which I am, and she is not. Zrinka was the only non-shifter in a house full of wolves. Everyone loved and respected her even if she called me a bitch and I couldn't reciprocate.

My eyes shot dagger-missiles at my sister. If they happened to deflect and pummel my father, I'd be good with that.

"Let's not start, girls," Dad said. "And Rink, don't keep giving that pup table scraps. He hasn't had his breakfast. The dog food is better for him."

"I would have been a late riser this morning with the rest of the pack, Reka." Dad turned to me. "If I didn't feel it necessary to talk with you."

Zrinka set a plate full of bacon and eggs on the table. Dad pulled it away from me and closer to him. He snagged a strip of bacon, bit off the end, and smiled at my sister's frown as she plunked down a basket of steamy biscuits where the eggs and bacon had been.

"Well, it would have been fine with me if you stayed in bed." I reached way over the table and grabbed a fist full of bacon and, very unlady-like but extremely wolf-like, bit off everything hanging over my thumb. I smiled and chomped instead of chewing with my mouth closed. "Coffee?" I asked, but it came out as 'offee?' with a little rise in pitch at the end. Almost like a Buddy whine.

Dad made large animal noises deep in his chest. As much as I would have loved continuing to push his buttons and revel in where that took us, I snagged my backpack off the rack by the pantry and shoved three biscuits inside. Then I kicked open the refrigerator for a pint of milk and headed for the back-screen door.

I breezed through the door and heard my sister say, "I don't know why you put up with her crap," and Dad answered, "Because she's just like her mother."

As a werewolf, my hearing was exemplary. If I wanted to tune in, I could have probably heard more, but Mondays were bad enough without starting them off with my family's feelings toward me.

I felt like I belonged in my laundry hamper with the rest of my soiled clothes as I ran across the yard.

THE HALLS AT REED CITY High were always noisy, cloying with too many scents, cluttered with students, and hard to navigate without making eye contact. But I was a pro since I'd done it for ten years. Back in my elementary school days, my dark eyes would turn gold if I got angry, frightened, or excited. Just like Dad, only he could control it when he needed to.

In junior high, I began to see more changes and became quite good at controlling the wolf in me. My sight, hearing, and sense of smell totally improved, so much that it hurt when navigating the noisy halls.

When I developed a keen feeling of knowing things like what was going to happen next, or how someone felt about me, or what they were thinking, and if they were Otherworld, Peter said it was wolf intuition. The only mythical creature I found hard to easily detect was the fae. They were amazing at masking everything and it took maturity and life experience to get a better grip on them.

I was one-third of the way down the hall before I saw Peter. He swaggered toward me, and I couldn't help but smile. If the whole stay at home and have kiddos didn't come between us, having him for a mate would've probably lasted forever. Reluctantly, I realized I might have to take his mark. That would put a dent in us being equals, and I feared it would taint the feelings we have for each other. A bite on my neck or shoulder would make me his property until death, and even worse, give us a strong bond to the pack.

Like this built-in thing that would enable Peter and the alphas in the pack to hone in on my location. At the moment, all I had was a smartphone and I could disable that and feel free to do as I like. A marked wolf had no freedom. Forever. That was a lifetime commitment.

"Man, I love a girl that smells like bacon in the morning," Peter said.

I spat a laugh; I couldn't help it. It just fell out of my mouth.

"I wasn't going to smile this morning," I said. "So, stop it." But it was what I loved about Peter. He always made me laugh.

"Yeah, I figured. I mean, not like you didn't run out on your dad last night. And by that look you just gave me, I bet he jumped on you at breakfast. If he did it's your fault. You know we were all supposed to be hunting that coyote pack together in—"

"Yeah. Right." I was not going to have another good day. Ever! "In some life celebratory, pack strength, hunt for survival kind of crap thing."

"The coyote pack is slowly killing off our food source on the property," Peter said, ignoring my drama. "We got seven of them last night. It was freaking awesome. You should've seen Zrinka when we all stomped into the kitchen." Peter laughed. "We were one bloody mess."

I think if your dad didn't insist your sister was homeschooled, she would be better off. I bet she'd love to lead a normal life, even enjoy attending high school. And Reka, she's the only one in this house who can have a normal life. Do you get that?"

"Yeah. I get it. As much as I get Zrinka living in a pack full of werewolves that hunt together when the moon is full, and come back all bloody, *is her real world*. There is an absolute chance Zrinka could have shifter kids with or without a shifter husband. She's my father's daughter, too."

Although my voice was very soft, my eyes jerked around the halls to see if anybody turned to look our way. And as always, no one seemed to care.

"Fat chance if she beds a human," Peter said. "But still, she can choose sterilization and a normal life. It's really not cool that she's stuck in the cabin all the time."

"She's protected there. And she loves taking care of the pack; she's gonna love playing little mommy to the kids, too. And really, it's all that she's got."

Peter's brow was furrowed, his eyes weepy. "Now maybe. But if she's willing to move far away, break ties with the pack and all shifters, she can live anywhere, be anything she sets her mind to. Best of all, she can have a relationship she can put first, before the pack."

Jade.

"Sometimes I wish I was her," I said.

And there it was. The reason I hated my sister. She could have anything she wished. But chose to be just like my mother. Mom chose the pack, too. And she died for it.

"You don't really mean that," Peter said. "You know you love the hunt, the way you see things, smell things, feel things. Your strength. And believe it or not, you've got a lot of freedom. There are different kinds of freedom, Reka."

I got it. I understood what he was getting at, but I didn't feel free. Not in my soul. I probably felt more trapped than Zrinka could ever imagine. I was a she-wolf in a pack full of boars that wanted to sire the next male alpha. Why couldn't I have had the opportunity to lead? I was an alpha, a natural born leader. Why hadn't I been trained since birth to step up? It wasn't fair. My only hope was to hang on to my independence and change the way bitches in the pack were treated. Then I would be allowed to challenge a pack leader for their title.

I tightened my jaw and gritted my teeth. "Speaking of humans ... or not. I hear we have a new kid at Lana's. Dave saw him at Vic's supermarket; said it looked like he was minding a couple of Otherworld kids from the foster home."

"Oh, hell yes! Woot!" Peter said and pumped his fist. "New blood from Down Under. Hope he's a shifter, not deep, dark, underworld weird, or untrustworthy like Jade, that fae guy at the gaming club. The one you seem to like way too much."

Crap!

"Man, I hope the new guy likes to hunt," Peter said, eyes roaming the halls.

"We're in Michigan. Who doesn't like to hunt?"

Chapter Four

CALASTAIR

I approached the local high school. It was a small and unimpressive building, like most on this planet. The surrounding trees showed colorful signs of decay. An occasional red or yellow leaf would tumble off one and be swept into the chilled air. Human teenagers swarmed the entrance, laughing, yelling, or commencing in insignificant conversation. I slipped in among them, trying my best not to draw attention.

The hallways were lined with metal lockers; apparently, each of the students had one assigned to them. I wondered if I had one, too. I flipped over the schedule Lana had given me, but it said nothing.

"Hey, copper top!" a voice came from behind me. I hoped it wasn't addressing me, but when I turned, I saw three of the students walking toward me. "Yo, you the new kid, huh?" the one in the middle asked. His hair was dark and smothered in some kind of product. "What's your name?"

"Cal," I answered, hoping this was the extent of his questions.

"Cal, huh? I'm Johnathan. This is Daniel and Tiffany." He gestured to a squatty boy with glasses and a big-eyed girl with blonde hair. Johnathan sized me up. "You sure stand out. Bright red hair, pale skin. Your parent Scottish or something?"

"...sure..." I said, wondering what exactly I had just agreed to. My eyes darted around, seeing if there was a way out of this conversation.

"Hey, relax man. I'm just joking with ya." He gave me a punch on the shoulder. "Got to be able to take a little teasing around here. Something ya got to know about us here in Reed City, we don't take things too seriously."

Something else to look forward to. "You guys a welcoming committee or something?"

Daniel laughed. "Nah. Just curious. Not a whole lot changes around here, so we just wanted to say hi."

"Oh, okay...hi."

"We're the band geeks," Tiffany said, blonde curls bouncing as she spoke. "You have an interest in joining? Geeks are cool nowadays ya know?"

I felt cornered. I hadn't expected to be included in anything, nor did I wish to be. All I was interested in was finding this girl so I could help her and get home. "Well, I don't know if I'll be here long enough to really join a group like that."

Johnathan nodded his head. "Ah. Family move around a lot then? It's cool; it's cool. Hey, if ya need anything, though, let us know."

A thought popped into my head; these three might be useful after all. Knowing so little about this place they could be a guide. "You know what, maybe you could help me. I was looking for a girl named Reka."

The three of them exchanged looks. "Why, you looking for her?" Daniel asked.

"Oh, uh..." My brain searched for a suitable answer. "Lana...I mean, my foster mom wanted me to tell her something. Guess they know each other," I lied.

Again, looks were exchanged. "Alright, alright, fair enough," Johnathan said. "She's pretty quiet but seems nice enough. Kind of a strange family, though."

My eyebrow raised. "Strange family...how so?"

"Well, that's kind of hard to explain. They keep to themselves in their house in the woods. They're always with a certain group of friends, real protective, and don't bother with the rest of us. Then there are stories about those woods..." Johnathan gave a laugh and a wave. "Ya know what, never mind, it's cool, I'm sure they're fine."

That sounded like something to follow up on, but Johnathan's reluctance on the subject made me think it was better to wait till later. "So, which one is Reka?"

Tiffany pointed toward the left side of the hallway. "She's the chick with purple streaks running through her dark hair. The one talking to Peter, Mr. tall, dark, and handsome himself."

I followed her gaze and found my mark. She was standing in front of her locker talking to a buff guy in black clothing. I watched how she carried herself. Her back was straight, and eyes focused on Peter, but they quickly darted away from other people in the hall.

A bell rang, and kids started to scatter to different rooms. "What the hell was that?" I asked.

Daniel looked at me with bemused eyes under his glasses. "What do you mean what was that? It's the five-minute warning bell. Time for class. What did the teachers do at your old school, yell at you to get out of the hall?"

"...yes..." I instantly kicked myself; I really needed to stop agreeing to stuff I didn't know about.

"Really? Wow. Okay," Daniel said. "We'll need to talk more about that later. Your old school sounds interesting."

"Yeah, but right now we gotta scramble," Johnathan said as the three started down the hall. "We got Mrs. Mackle for English, and she's a Nazi for tardies. Catch ya later."

I gave them a polite wave as they turned away. They were pathetically needy but seemed like good people. Not that it really mattered at the moment. I wasn't here to make friends. I looked around and saw Reka's dark hair disappear into room 103. Good. That was the first-class Lana had me down for, Advanced Algebra.

I walked into the classroom and quickly spotted Reka and Peter sitting at the back table. I hurried to slide into the seat next to her before anyone else could. She was too caught up in conversation with Peter to notice.

Alright, I thought, mentally cracking my knuckles. *Let's get this show on the road.*

"Hi there! I'm Cal," I said, trying to mimic the excitement Johnathan, Tiffany, and Daniel showed.

Reka turned toward me, eyebrows raised. "Oh, hey. I'm Reka, this is Peter. You're the new kid, right?"

"Yup, just moved in."

"You like Reed City so far?"

"Not at all," I responded before I could think. "Sorry. I mean...it's an adjustment. I grew up in a big city, ya know, like, really big. I'm sure I'll get used to its, oh I don't know, quaintness?"

Reka narrowed her eyes a little. "Okaaaaay."

I wondered for a moment if I had insulted her, but figured it was best to push forward. But I struggled to figure out anything useful to say. "So, you any good at math?" finally fumbled out of my mouth.

She gave a small shrug as a response. Her attention seemed to be trying to waver off me just like I tried to get away from the 'geeks' in the hall.

"Alright." I tapped my finger against the desk, trying to pull forth any ideas from my brain as to how to reach this girl. "Oh, I know, tell me about yourself Reka. What kinds of things do you like to do? How are things at home?"

Reka's eyes turned into a full-fledged frown. "Wow, creep much? Look, I don't know what your deal is but if you're trying to flirt or something, you got a lot of work to do."

"Flirt? Eww!" I said as the words left my mouth faster than I could stop them again.

"What do you mean eww?!" she hissed.

Peter half rose from his seat. "Hey, have some respect!"

"I didn't...I mean...No. Wait. That's not what I meant..." Words were just falling from my lips now as I quickly tried to diffuse the situation. "I'm just trying to get to know you."

Reka rolled her eyes and turned her back toward me to face Peter.

I wondered if somewhere up in heaven, my father was laughing.

Chapter Five

R EKA

Jeeze, who the heck was this guy? He thought our town was quaint but hated it here, and, when I shrugged off the math question, his comeback was 'tell me about yourself? How are things at home?' Weird, weird, weird. Him staying at Lana's was enough reason to be cautious. He paid very little attention to Peter and seemed to be trying to find out something about Dad or me. Why?

Mrs. Tanner was grading homework at her desk in the front of the room. The rest of the class worked quietly on an assignment, while Cal, the alien, shot me thoughtful glances. He had two pencils. One actively working the task, the other tucked behind his ear. His movements were jerky. I smelled tension, and it drew me to him like a wounded bunny in an open field.

He was kind of cute with his bright red hair, stormy gray eyes, and perpetual frown. His skin was a little too pale. Pale was typical for Michiganders, but Cal's skin almost glowed—surreal. I should have asked him where he was from. A big city boy from California would be tan even if he hated the outdoors. Cal was not human and had an odd smell. I couldn't place it. His clothes screamed 'I don't play in the woods'.

Mine probably screamed 'I live in a cave' and preferred it that way by the statement on my tee shirt. *Close*, I thought with an inner chuckle. He apparently didn't want to be here, by the pheromones he was shooting off. And that sent up more than one red flag. Our meeting could be pack related, and he sure didn't smell like a wolf. The attempt to make conversation, although forced, seemed driven, not merely to be pleasant.

I stole a glance. He hopped on it and gave me a quick squinty-eyed smile. Forced.

Peter was busy working the assignment. I watched his long fingers push the pencil along the words and numbers on the page, efficiently working the problem on scratch paper before he copied it carefully onto the worksheet. Ugh, it aggravated me. Peter was so good at math. He always received high grades in everything, even in elementary school. But right now, I felt the wolf in him. It simmered with a strong desire to put himself between alien-guy and me.

I looked away, tried to concentrate on the assignment, but my mind kept wandering to the redhead sitting too close for comfort. The whole situation hadn't felt right. Cal had walked in, scanned the room, and then made his way to the back of the room and sat right next to me. There were at least a dozen vacant chairs in front of us. He'd singled me out. No doubt.

I gritted my teeth. This had better not be my father's doing. That was a viable option.

Having a wolf under my skin, always waiting to immerge, gave me a naturally curious nature. Being an alpha female added a thick layer of pack protection I wasn't comfortable with.

Meeting a new Otherworld being this way reminded me that there was always someone higher on the food chain, and because I was a she-wolf, capable of childbearing, everyone was in danger if I was. I hated that.

It was warm in the classroom and sitting between two guys didn't help. Both were giving off way too much body heat. Wolves didn't do confinement well, especially when it gets closer to winter and every freaking establishment cranks up the heat. This room did not offer a good view of outdoors to take my mind off it, either. It was a half-basement room with very few windows. The ones it did have were up high on one wall, a thin runner of grass between me and the outside walkway. All I could see was the occasional passersby's knees and sky.

A constant and low rumble got my attention, and Peter's ... until I realized it was me. I was doing everything I could to stay calm. But my wolf wanted out. I swallowed her rumble and stared at Peter with a desperate need to get out of here.

Peter furrowed his brow and continued to work but slid his arm closer until our elbows connected.

I didn't move my arm and glanced around the room. Everyone was quiet and busily working on the assignment Mrs. Tanner had given us, or the homework she had put up on the chalkboard. And she was still making check marks on whatever was on her desk. The sounds of pencils on paper, feet shuffling on wood floors, and the occasional cough or crumpled paper was electric if I concentrated on it. A flash of pain shot behind my eyes with each mild disruption.

I took in a deep breath. Peter would be feeling my angst, and no doubt mention it tonight at dinner. I hated the tight bond we had even without his mark. It generated from our brand to our leader, my father. Mine given at birth, Peter's also. Others received it during a welcoming ceremony when they joined the pack, or through marriage. If you marry into a pack, approval is automatic. All wolves were allowed to pick a mate of their choosing when ready, except me. And that thought made me growl noticeably.

Peter moved closer.

Cal's eyes fell on my assignment sheet, and then traveled to my tee shirt. Pretty sure it wasn't my boobs his eyes roamed after that 'ewe' comment.

I was rewarded when his lips moved slightly as he read **Will you just stop talking** and then he quickly turned back to his worksheet.

Alien-boy continued shooting what I was sure he thought were inconspicuous side glances in my direction. I disliked unwanted attention, especially from someone that didn't smell altogether human. I tried to shake it off until I could talk to Peter. But at this point, I was kinda pretty sure Cal was alien. He smelled Otherworld, but not like he was from Down Under. We didn't often run into Otherworld creatures we couldn't quickly identify, but it was often enough to warrant concern, yet we must respect the anonymity of the situation. The town was crawling with us freakazoids. I never asked, never pushed, unless it was necessary. Man, I hoped Cal wasn't in any more of my classes.

Later, when I shoved my Algebra book back inside my locker, Peter asked about Cal, "Did you smell Otherworld on the weird redheaded kid?"

I wasn't shocked he beat me to it. Wolves have a great ability to sense as well as smell.

"Yeah. You get a handle on what? He's not a shifter," I said.

"Nope, too unearthly, possibly fae. But there's something safe about him, like the crisp air in the early morning, light and sunny, like the woods in the summer. So, I don't think he's too dangerous. I didn't like him getting close to you, though."

Peter didn't like Jade getting close either. He said it was because Jade was fae. That guy-girl protection thing doesn't work with two alphas. It screws up my feelings for him. I hate that part of him. I'm perfectly capable of taking care of myself.

I frowned. "Cal—he has a name—didn't hit on me. He went all wacko at the thought of me thinking he did. Maybe he was trying to hit on you," I said with a smile.

Peter rolled his eyes. "I was too freaked out to notice," Peter said. "Even so, wacko-guy was interested in *something* about you. I think we need to find out what."

"Can we not mention this to Dad? Let's just downplay the new kid if anyone asks until we see if Cal hits me or you up again, okay?"

"Maybe we can tell your father it's your sexy-self he's really interested in, but he was Otherworld, awkward, and bumbled the whole thing up," Peter joked. "Your dad will love that. End of story."

"You're kidding, right? Like I so want to tell my dad some redheaded new kid that smells Otherworld flirted with me in Algebra class today." I pushed Peter against his open locker door as hard as one of the football players could. "When her clearly didn't!"

"Okay! Fine!" Peter said. "I just hope if he was flirting—-he grinned at me—with either of us he got the message and backs off until we can figure out what he is."

"Oh, so you're interested." I joked and it was his turn to push me into the lockers. I bounced off with a grin on my face.

The crazy rush to get to the next class before the second bell had kids spitting lude or taunting remarks at us as we bickered and laughed at each other. We always avoided attention; never engaged in confrontation like Peter just did. Cal seemed to bring out the worst in Peter. When he glared at the passing crowd, then leaned in and pecked me on the cheek, I almost slapped him but that would have just given the crowd another opportunity for an unwanted response.

Peter's lips were close to my ear. "It's taken us years to establish we don't care to play with humans, keep to ourselves like the Amish around here, and your father and the other packs put that kind of behavior high on their priority list. So, kidding aside, if Cal keeps it up, we need to do something."

I pushed Peter away and punched him in the arm. "Will you shut up?! You just got more attention in the three minutes we've been fooling around by our lockers!"

I mimicked his eye roll. "The whole conversation with Cal during class got zilch from anyone but you," I said as I added a spiral notebook to my pile. And new-guy walked out before we did."

I glanced at the crowd; they were passing at a normal pace that quickly accelerated at the sound of the first bell. Five minutes until class time, add another two or three to be seated...I was going to be late.

"Look." I lowered my voice and pushed back the books still in my locker as I talked. "Maybe Cal smelled Otherworld on us," I quietly hissed, "and was looking for some friendship. You ever think of that? Don't you wonder what it would be like to have real friends out of our circle? I sure do."

"Well, that's an about-face from the way you were stressing back there. I'm surprised others didn't question your growls. But, hey, you want to befriend the 'wacko'—" Peter's fingers quoted. "—Go right ahead. What harm can it do?" His lips forced a smile.

Swell! I had two classes before lunch, both on the other side of the school. I slammed the locker door, spun the lock, and turned to leave.

Peter snagged my arm. "I won't see you until lunch."

"Ah, duh? Like I don't know that," I said, and pulled my arm away.

"It was a warning. Don't be stupid. Try talking to someone in the pack about making Otherworld friends. Maybe another opinion would help change your mind. And if that doesn't work, maybe you should ask your father if you can stay in Big Rapids with one of other packs for a while. At least I know you would be protected under the tri-county treaty."

"I'm pissed with my fate in life, not vindictive," I said through a clenched jaw. "I'll work it out. By myself. I don't need a redheaded guy's shoulder to cry on, or a wolf pack to protect me."

Chapter Six

CALASTAIR

Classes were dry and uneventful. I jotted down notes and did the work, but the lectures were so boring I didn't bother paying much attention. Not like I was down here to get good grades, anyway. My mind constantly wandered to my first encounter with Reka. Part of me wondered if I could ever recover from such an awful start. Not only did I manage to insult her, but I made myself look like a damn fool.

The bell rang for lunch period. Students rushed down the hallway, gleeful for any amount of time out of the classroom. I made my way to the cafeteria through the commotion of slamming lockers and screaming humans.

The lunchroom served something called macaroni and cheese. Even though I knew nothing about the human's cuisine, I doubted what they had was the best quality. The gelatinous orange blob oozed over the tray like watery mucous. How could a human look at this and decide they wanted it in their body?

Scanning the lunchroom, I quickly spotted Reka. She sat at a corner table by herself, eyes lowered at her tray as she picked at the macaroni. My thumb tapped the side of my tray. Did I really want to try talking to her again so soon? The last attempt was such a disaster; I contemplated giving a little time before talking to her again. Of course, the longer I waited, the longer I had to stay on this plane of existence. Impatience won out.

I took a deep breath and weaved my way through students to Reka's table. *Be cool, man*, I thought to myself. *Remember, I don't have to solve all her problems right away. Let's just talk to her and not make an ass of yourself. That'd be a good start.* I swung into the seat across from her.

Reka looked up expectantly, but her expression dropped when she saw me. "Oh, you're back, huh?"

It wasn't quite the response I was hoping for. "Yeah. Look...I wanted to apologize. I might have come on a bit strong when we first talked. I'm just, you know, not used to this whole talking to people thing."

Reka's eyes scanned my face. She brushed stray black hair behind her ear. "I guess I can understand that. Word to the wise, best to avoid people when you can. They kind of suck."

Lady, you have no idea. But this is a good start, what's next? I let my instincts kick in. Angels were natural empaths, and even though I was only half angel, my ability was still potent. She sat alone, eyes down, avoiding any stray student that walked past. However, she wasn't terribly standoffish when talked to directly. *A bit of a loner, but maybe she doesn't want to be deep down?* I could use that.

"Well, anyway. Let's start again. Hi, I'm Cal, and I am incredibly uncomfortable in this school, and awkward."

Reka chortled. "Well, I'm Reka. And ditto."

I smiled. This was going much better than it had last time. I was so pleased with myself that when I saw her shovel a spoonful of macaroni into her mouth, I followed suit. And instantly regretted it when I realized I had no idea what to do then. Angels didn't need to eat on our plane. I sat there with the orange goo in my mouth, rolling it around my tongue, trying to figure out what to do with it. I watched Reka move her lower jaw around, so I mimicked her. The macaroni was still there, just ground into a slightly more disgusting material. I saw her muscles in her neck contract to swallow. It took a few unsuccessful attempts, but, eventually, I figured it out and got it down.

I took a deep breath. "Oh, that was horrifying."

"Yeah," she said. "They always make it too tangy. But you'll get used to it."

I was about to tell her I meant the whole experience but caught myself. I knew my body on Earth would need nutrients, but until I got used to it, the bare minimum would have to do.

"So, I heard you live with Lana in her foster home," Reka said. "She's got a few screws loose, but she's nice."

"I have yet to figure her out, but yeah, she doesn't seem too bad."

"How did you end up there?" she said, and instantly looked like she regretted it. "Oh, sorry, it's fine if you don't want to talk about it."

I swallowed another mouthful of the orange monstrosity. "It's okay. Just complicated, though." I started pushing the food around my tray nervously. "Well, quite a few years back my mom passed away and my dad and I never saw eye to eye. He's..." My mind sifted, trying to find a good term. "...a soldier. He left for a mission, so he sent me here."

Reka eyed me with doubt. "I didn't know they sent kids to foster homes for that."

"Yeah, well, these are kind of unique circumstances. Like I said, it's complicated. Anyway, it's fine. I could use a break from the old man anyway."

Reka continued to watch me, and I struggled down another bite. "Well, I get that feeling. Sometimes listening to my dad is like throwing a handful of nails into a blender and leaving the lid off."

"Really?" My ears perked up. Maybe this could be something to help explain my mission here.

"Yeah, he's so controlling. Sometimes I just like to waltz on the edge of his temper to keep him pissed off."

"Right on!" I realized I had a smile on my face again, but this time it wasn't pretend. It was the first time I had ever heard anyone question their father like I had. "It's fun sometimes, isn't it? To know where that line is and just poke at it but not cross."

"Until you do."

"That just lets you know where it is, so you don't the next time," I said, my mother's mischievous grin crossing my face. I hadn't thought I'd find people down here that I'd actually relate to. Perhaps my dad made a mistake sending me here and this wasn't going to suck after all.

A shadow crept over the table between us. I looked up to see Peter glaring at me over his lunch tray.

"Everything alright here?" Peter asked Reka.

"Oh, it's fine. You can sheath that stare. Cal and I were just bonding over our mutual dislike for our fathers."

"I see." Peter didn't look happy at my presence but sat next to Reka.

I couldn't help noticing his imposing frame and wondered if he used it often to intimidate people. Our conversations changed from home life, to school work, and to the town. The whole time I sensed a certain distaste from Peter. He hid it well, but my empathic abilities detected it. It was a potential problem if he tried to convince Reka not to talk to me. But by the end of the lunch period, I felt there was a friendly connection between us. And that was a success.

Chapter Seven

R<u>EKA</u>
  I smiled at Peter as Cal tried to make conversation. I could tell Peter was not happy. I suppose I should have discouraged Cal from joining me. Instead, I shared my issues with Dad. Anything personal within the pack was forbidden information to outsiders. I broke several rules by letting Cal sit down with me—definitely in for some crap. Double crap if Dad questioned Peter about our day.

I tilted my head, raised my eyebrows, and give Peter a smile that said, be nice.

Kids close to our table were staring, probably because they had never seen me this friendly. When Peter arrived, others in the room began scrutinizing us unbeknown to Calastair. I could understand Peter's concern. I opened a door the pack locked years ago.

As I boldly ran my eyes over the lunchroom, I noticed it was more quiet than usual. And when my gaze grazed, heads turned away and conversations looked forced. I even noticed a few cell phones out. Texts, rumors, camera shots flying?

Crap.

Otherworld creatures would wonder if Cal was pack. Humans would wonder what made Cal so special that we accepted him.

Double Crap.

I never really thought of consequences since I had no desire to mingle in the past.

For some reason, the whole thing really pissed me off. I should have the right to connect with anyone I wanted. Dad connected with townspeople, for thwarting suspicion and conducting business he would say.

I watched the new student's enthusiasm with Peter, his complete unawareness of what was happening around him, and realized I needed to warn him. No. I needed to stop encouraging him. I could not poke a hornet's nest and expect no response.

Peter and Cal were up and gathered their trays. The sounds in the room rose briefly. I ignored them, and my common sense.

"So, Cal, what's your next class?" I stood and asked.

Cal dug a white card out of his pants pocket and studied it as we moved through the lunchroom. He didn't seem to notice the waves of silence, followed by enthusiastic chatter as we passed clusters of students. But Peter did and kept shooting me tight eyes over a furrowed brow.

"Biology. Room 113. Mr. Cutts," Cal said. "I assume it's on the south side of campus. I pulled the text book out of my locker just in case."

The first bell sounded, and we automatically stepped up our pace.

"You assumed right," Peter said. He pointed toward a door near the end of the lunchroom. "Take a left through the double doors."

When Cal turned to check out the door, Peter shot me a set of angry eyebrows. "Hold up, Reka."

I ignored him. "Cal, I have biology now, too!" But Peter knew that. "I'll walk with you."

"That's great!" Cal said.

As I stepped up beside Cal. "We can talk later, Peter. I don't want Cal to be late to his first class with Cutts."

"We wouldn't want that." Peter's lips curled back in a snarl. The kids heading out of the lunchroom gave him a wide berth.

"Then it's settled," I said. "You're going to like Mr. Cutts. He's amusing and easy to work with. Last week, he talked about deer crap for twenty minutes. Literally. See, the deer eat apples and then they wander—deer have a tendency to stay in the same area, but their territory can be a mile or two wide, or more—and then they poop out the apple seeds, and whallah! A new tree is born."

Standing next to a disposal bin for lunch trays, Peter vibrated like an old window fan. He put his tray down hard enough to rattle the silverware.

"That is ... very interesting," Cal said through a lopsided grin.

I was having a hard time judging his reaction, but it sure was fun to watch Peter all frazzled. I winked at him and mouthed, *I got this*. Peter didn't look amused.

"I'll catch you after phys ed," Peter said.

With a friendly smile, Cal asked Peter, "What's Fizz Ed?"

"It's physical education," I said before Peter could answer. "I got stuck with dance this quarter. But it's more like aerobics to country music. I hate it. Peter has weight training. I put in for weight training, but guys get in first."

Cal was staring at his schedule. "I have dance class, too." He didn't look happy. "Last period."

Peter snickered.

Dancing with the new guy. Ugh! I mentally saw myself leaning on a shovel and looking into a dark hole. "Cool!" I said. "At least I'll have someone else to suffer with!"

Crap! That sounded way too exuberant.

"Well, that's something," Cal said. He took in a deep breath and let it out slowly.

"You two have fun." Peter smiled at me. "I'll see you in civics, fifth period."

Pulling up his schedule like he hoped it was a winning lottery ticket, Cal said, "I don't have civics this semester."

"Well, that's something," Peter said sarcastically with a friendly knuckle poke to the redhead's bicep. "Catch you later, man."

Peter—my supposedly mate to be—headed out the closest exit without making eye contact again.

From inside that hole I had dug, I could see mounds of dirt falling from above, and Peter's smiling face.

Cal and I moved around a crowd lingering by the lunchroom back door—which I totally ignored—as he asked, "Is Peter your boyfriend?"

I didn't know how to answer that, so like everything else I did today, I winged it. "It would make my father smile if he were. He's a close friend of the family, spends a lot of time at our place. We grew up together. So, I guess you could say he's my best friend."

There. No lies. I felt proud of myself.

The students were gawking, cell phones in hands. I saw myself digging the six feet rectangle a little deeper.

A blonde girl—with breasts I should have been born with—stepped out of a group and blocked the exit. I'd seen blondie around since junior high but still didn't know her name. And I wasn't about to ask now.

"Do you finally have a boyfriend, Reka?" perky boobs asked and pointed at Cal.

The group of football players, cheerleaders, and wannabees snickered behind and beside itty-bitty perky boobs. I smiled.

Cal said, "Nah, I just like her tee shirt." He pointed to the words **Will you just stop talking** stretched across my bulbous mounds.

Half the group spit laughs.

Cal didn't seem to notice his words had double meaning.

I slapped on some snarky lips and said, "Alright everyone, give it up. I thought since the Junior High incident everyone got it. I don't do guys."

Lips parted; jaws dropped.

Guess not. I grabbed for Cal's hand and yelped from a sharp, static shock. I snagged his shirt and pulled him toward the door before he could do something else stupid. Where did alien-guy's father keep him for most of his life?

"The others looked quite perplexed," Cal said as the door slid shut behind us. "Would you mind catching me up on the Junior High incident you neglected to expand on back there?"

"Yeah. No. I just made that crap up."

"I don't understand. Why?" Cal asked.

I stared at him for a moment before answering. The guy really didn't have a clue.

"Well," I finally said. "If guys think I prefer girls, and girls are totally into the guys, it means I don't have to worry about a prom date this year. Probably not next year either."

Now he looked totally confused. Alien, my mind sung.

I decided to change the subject. "You said your father is a soldier on a mission. Is he, like, in some special service kind of field operative position with the government or something?"

Cal's eyes blinked several times before answering. "Kind of. But I'm not allowed to talk about it."

Okay. So now he was just plain evasive. I felt beyond a doubt the guy was Otherworld. All I had to do was find out what I was dealing with. Why was this otherwise natural talent so difficult? I wanted to growl.

"Oh." I said sweetly, "Is your dad abusive, too?" as we sidled around eleventh graders rushing to beat the second bell. "And you have no family to talk to or stay with when he's on a mission?"

I swore Cal shrunk two inches before answering. "Uh. No. He's not abusive just exasperating at times. And there are no relatives that could be effective in keeping me ... hidden. And since I need an adult guardian—"

I put up my hand. He glanced down at it. "Got it," I said. "So, you ended up with Lana and her bunch of misfits."

"I wouldn't call them misfits. I'm certainly not a misfit," Cal said and opened the door to room 113.

He was lying through his misfit, Otherworldly teeth. And if it's not so, I totally was never going to trust my superpowers again.

Chapter Eight

C ALASTAIR

The rest of the day was uneventful. One class after another with lectures, homework, complaining teenagers, rinse and repeat. The only exception was dance class. I found it a strange concept to be taught in school. Angels danced, of course, but it was very formal. The way humans danced was...erratic. The moves were quick and without elegant motion. Added to that, I was the only male in the class. It made me rather uncomfortable.

Strangely, though, Reka's company made it tolerable. We talked and joked between breaks. She seemed very different than the other humans. Most looked at me strangely and with judging eyes, but she didn't. Sure, I still got a little vibe of suspicion off some of her questions. But I didn't blame her for that. I was, after all, still new to her. But by the end of the day, I found I laughed along with her, and I didn't even have to fake it.

I walked home, proud of myself. I didn't know yet how I was supposed to help Reka, but I took major steps toward my mission completion. Earning her trust was imperative to my goal. I just hoped that friend of hers, Peter, didn't mess anything up. Toward the end of our lunch period he wasn't even trying to hide his dislike for me. I could sense he had a strong, controlling personality. And I could even detect a ping of jealousy every time Reka talked with me. I wondered if he was whispering words of poison about me into her ear right now.

As I entered my earth home, I was welcomed by loud, blaring music. The chaotic drums beat so loud I could feel them in my chest. Holding my hands to my ears to block the atrocious sounds, I searched where it came from. I found Lana in the living room, her head thrashing to the beat. The brown curls on her head snapping around a second after her skull's movement. Her eyes widened with surprise as I approached, and she hurried to shut the music off.

"Sorry, dear," she said through the ringing in my ears. "All the kids were out playing, so I was just enjoying some down time."

"What level of Hell's fiery inferno did you drag that music from?"

"It's called heavy metal. Guess they probably don't have much of that in heaven, do they?"

I buried my head in my hands, trying to quell the instant headache the music produced. "No, in fact they don't, thank the father. How can you listen to that?"

Lana shrugged. "I find the melodies relaxing."

"You call that relaxing?! You know, in a house full of strange creatures, you may be the strangest."

A toothy grin popped on her face. "To someone like me, that's a compliment, Calastair."

"Whatever." I slung my backpack on the floor and plopped myself into one of the living room chairs. My muscles were achy and tired, another new sensation. But the cushion on the chair cradled me. I felt I could stay there the rest of my life. I closed my eyes and snuggled my head into the headrest.

"How was your first day of school?" Lana's voice asked from beyond my eyelids.

"Actually, pretty great," I said. "Classes were dull, but I managed to make a good connection with Reka. Think she considers me a friend now. Should figure out how to help her soon and be on my way."

"Really?!"

I opened my eyes and propped my head up on my arm to look at her, the bright flowered housedress she wore assaulted my eyes. "You don't have to sound so surprised."

"Surprised? I'm astonished! Didn't really expect you to stay in school the whole day, let alone make a friend."

"Wow. I see now why the angels have you look after runaway children. Your warmth and encouraging personality must be the thing of legend."

Lana winked. "I'm always honest, dear. You left this morning in a snit; wasn't sure if you were going to take it seriously. I was rooting for you, though."

A bright flash and a swirl of flame erupted. The two children with red hair appeared through a portal and tore upstairs, chasing one another.

Lana sighed. "Well, the twins are up. Guess break time is over." She poked my bag with uncomfortable looking pointed shoes. "Why don't you get some homework done? I'll call you down when dinner is ready."

Oh yay, I thought, *I can't wait to shove more glop down my gullet.* I eased myself forward as my body protested leaving the comfort of the chair. "Spent the whole day in class, then have to spend the evening on more work. How do these humans ever find time to actually live their short lives?"

"They are very talented," she said, turning to follow the twins. "Do you need any help with your homework?"

I let out a laugh. "I'm three hundred and fifty years old. I've seen more than any human will in their lifetime. I think I can handle a little paperwork."

WHAT THE HELL IS AN imaginary number? If it's imaginary, why is it in the equation?!

I chucked the math book onto the cluttered floor in frustration. *What does it matter anyway? Math isn't going to help me with Reka.*

My mind wandered to her. She was contradictory. Reka said she was a loner, and so did other people. Yet, she was welcoming of my company. She also didn't seem like a shy person who was afraid to speak up, so why barricade herself?

For a moment, I thought of Peter and wondered if his protective attitude could be keeping her from branching out. But Reka had a strong personality. I couldn't see her bending to anyone's will like that.

I closed my eyes and thought of our conversations. I used my empathic abilities to scan every word I could remember with every facial tick, physical reaction, and expression that went with them. For all her strength, there was vulnerability. There was a secret she was hiding, something suffocating. Something she could not fight on her own. And I could hear it in her tone of voice, especially when she talked about her family, that she was trapped. Her control was being taken away, and she could not fight it, but why? Could it be fear? No. That didn't seem right. Loyalty maybe? One thing was becoming clear to me, though. I was going to need to spend more time talking to Reka. Surprisingly, I didn't mind the idea, and was actually looking forward to it.

A knock came at my door. I swiveled my chair around to see Lana.

"Some kids from school are here. They said they were your friends," she said. "How'd you become so popular in one day?"

"I have no idea." Confused, I stood and walked toward her. "Did you get their names?"

"Yeah, a Daniel, Tiffany, and Johnathan."

The names sounded familiar. It took me a moment to remember them from the beginning of the school day. "The Geek Squad? What are they here for?" I chuckled. "Geek Squad. That was pretty funny. Wonder if anyone came up with that before."

"Oh, sweetie." Lana ruffled the hair on the back of my head. "You could be the wittiest Angel in heaven, but down here you're a step or two behind."

I scowled and brushed her hand away. "What do they want?"

"I don't know. I'm your caretaker, not your receptionist," Lana said as she turned and walked away.

I hurried to the front door and saw Daniel, Tiffany, and Johnathan waiting on the front porch, talking and laughing. As I approached, their attention instantly turned toward me.

"Hey man! How's it going?" Johnathan bellowed.

"Yeah, I'm good. What're you guys doing here?"

"Just cruising around the area, thought we'd swing by, see how your first day went."

"Oh, that's nice." The words felt flat, and I feared insincere.

We stood there awkwardly for a few seconds until Tiffany pointed through the threshold. "Can we come in?"

"Uh..." I peeked behind the door that thankfully blocked the other three's view. I saw a five-year-old with blue hair jumping on the couch. He let out a belch that erupted in flame. Lana franticly chased after the twins, her furry tail flickering behind her. "Nah. It's pretty crazy in there. Let's just hang out on the porch."

We found three chairs. The white paint was weathered and chipping off the metal. I had wondered if the poor support would be able to hold my weight. It wobbled but held.

Johnathan leaned his lanky frame against the house's siding. "You made kind of a buzz around school, sitting with Reka and Peter at lunch. Usually, they don't let people near them."

Reka wasn't a topic I particularly wanted to talk to them about. "Yeah, well like I said, Lana knows her."

Daniel leaned forward; his chair creaked under his heavier build. "So, does that mean she knows Reka's parents? Did Lana tell you what their deal is?"

I frowned. "What do you mean?"

Tiffany patted Daniel's knee. "What he meant, lacking tactfulness, of course, was do you know what they are like? We see her every day at school. But outside of it they're very secretive. Pretty much just see them at the store for supplies. But they're kind of spooks as far as the town is concerned."

I absorbed the information. "Well, she hasn't said anything about them. But I'm curious now. Do you know anything else?"

Johnathan laughed. "Not really, but it's not like we've really tried to find out either. Just kind of interesting. Every town has their weirdos, I guess. I do know that her father has quite a temper, though. Doesn't take much to set him off so be careful if you meet him."

"Good to know, thanks."

Another mention of the father. I was detecting a pattern.

Daniel reached into his bag and pulled out four bottles filled with green liquid. He passed one to me. "Here. I picked ya up one."

"Oh, uh...thanks," I said and took it. I wasn't really sure what it was for until I saw the other three open theirs and drink it.

Oh great, yet another thing to cram into my stomach. These people are obsessed with it.

I opened the bottle and heard a fizzing sound. Trying not to be rude, I took a quick swig. Bubbles sparked in my throat like little pin pricks. But after that passed a flavor washed over my tongue. It was completely different from the abhorred lunch I had. This actually was good. Really good.

"What is this? It's amazing!"

Tiffany's eyebrow raised. "You never had *Mountain Dew* before?"

"No. It's awesome, though. What mountain did it come from?"

The three looked at each other, seemingly at a loss for words.

"Dude. Really?" Johnathan asked.

I wasn't sure what I had said wrong. "I'm just kidding," I backtracked.

They smiled. "Good. I thought for a second you were out of your mind or something," Johnathan said with a laugh. "We should probably get going, though; parents want me home by dinner."

They stood up and each gave their well wishes as they left. I wondered why they were being so friendly with me. After all, we had just met this morning, and I wasn't exactly warm to them. Watching them walk away, I realized something that surprised me. I kind of liked them.

Chapter Nine

R^{EKA} "You're wrong. Cal's different," I said, and watched Peter's eyes turn cold.

"No shit. My point exactly. And that matters. You don't start chatting it up with somebody you don't really know. Down Under, yakking it up is safer. At least you know what you're dealing with because we're free to be us down there. But above ground, what if you get carried away, tell someone you love the moon because it brings out the beast in you, and the beast loves fresh meat?

"Making friends, getting close, starting a lasting relationship; that's a pack decision up here where we're trying to keep what we are secret. And speaking of friends, did you even notice your new friend had the Geek Squad's attention today? Like all freakin' day. I followed Daniel, Tiffany, and Johnathan after school. Guess where they ended up?"

Peter was on a rant. I sighed. Better to let him play it out. "Okay. I'll bite. Where?"

"Lana's. Cal gave the trio a good reason to cross the street, since you and alien guy were so chummy today. They jumped on it. They never had reason to graduate from the park across the street. Everyone from Down Under knows those three have suspicions about some of us and that's why they watch Lana's. Tiffany led them up to the front door, and I watched while they chatted with Cal right on Lana's front porch.

"Come on, Reka. Be real. Those kids don't sit under that big oak with their laptops to do homework. So far, the council has ignored the three snoops, but if they get too close, Lana will have to send a vamp to mind wipe. And if your father finds out you're the reason they got too close..." Peter shook his head and picked up his pace. "At least they're afraid to venture into our woods."

"You done?" I asked.

Peter raked a hand through his black hair. His irises had small rings of gold flashing the rims. His wolf was near the surface.

A breeze rattled overhead, and red, gold, and umber colored leaves floated down on the path before us. It softened my tight lips as I silently walked and waited for Peter's response.

"Fine. Be that way," Peter said. "But if you think this guy is someone you want that close you need to bring it up at the next meeting. And if you don't, I may have a talk with Raz or Papo about this. My suggestion would be to tell them we know he's Otherworld up front."

I stole a glance as we moved along. Peter's nostrils flared, and he puffed out a frustrated sigh. "At least find out what he is tomorrow before the meeting," he said and raked hair off his forehead with his fingers. "Get him to expand on why he's here. I'd do that way before bringing him home to meet Dakota."

"Don't be acting like you're all smart instead of just plain jealous," I spat. "And don't you dare threaten me with going to Raz or Papo, either. You know I wouldn't do any of that crap. I'm not stupid. Right now, my father doesn't need to know anything about Cal. Give me a break, Peter, or I may just go rogue. I can bunk at Lana's, you know. She may not know me well, but she's sympathetic. I'm old enough to deal with my life on my own. Got it?"

Peter looked smug. "Well, you're damn sure not acting like it. We just met this guy today. I don't get it. Is it some love at first sight thing?"

I didn't know how to answer. Was it a physical attraction? No! The guy got me, though. He understood the dad thing. Plus, I could talk to him. But really, if I had to be honest, he was not pack. Plain and simple. And lately, I was all anti-pack. I scuffed along, purposely ignoring the 'love at first sight' stupidity.

I kicked a piece of dead wood. Fallen leaves rolled over my tennis shoes and ankles as we walked. The woods on our property were backlit by a sinking sun. It was so vivid it took my breath away. Fall was my favorite time of year. The color, smells, and sounds made the wolf in me whimper to be released.

"I haven't said a single thing to Calastair about who or what we are," I said. "And I don't intend to until I know what he is. We only talked about school, dance class, life at Lana's, and issues with controlling fathers; something we share."

"Yeah, well, that right there is the problem. You have no right telling anyone about us unless you get pack approval, and you know it. The only time we let others in is if they knock on the cabin door by invitation. Even then, it's an alpha leader's decision. What you're doing is almost always followed by a council cleansing. And you know the work involved in that. And the penalty. Your father won't be too keen on owing vampires, fairies, or witches for your stupid moves."

"Rules-rules-rules. It's always about rules. I thought when we became adults, we'd have the right to make our own decisions. Humans do. And we're higher on the food chain than them, blood-lust predators, monsters kids want dads to spook out from under their beds and out of closets after dark."

I bent to pick up a rock the size of a chicken egg, only flat, slate-colored. The weight was comfortable in my hand. I rubbed it on my jeans until it felt smooth on my palm.

"Look, Peter," I softly said. "I feel like I can talk to Calastair without pack rules getting in the way. He's a nice guy. He doesn't howl at the moon. At least I don't think he does. And having a friend that doesn't have an agenda that's in my father's best interest is a gift."

Peter stopped abruptly and turned toward me. I brazenly glared. A menacing growl burbled in my throat. He tightened his mouth and dimples popped under his cheeks. I felt butterflies in the pit of my stomach that softened my rumbling wolf...until he opened his mouth.

"Man, Reka! That's exactly what I'm afraid of—what I've been talking about. I thought you said you didn't discuss the pack. Talking about your dad in a negative way is the pack."

"No it's not!" *That sounded snotty.* I winced. Peter's dimples didn't stop the wolf in me from going on. "Every kid has a father, human or not, Peter."

Low blow. Peter did not know who is family was. But he was making me angry.

"And there's nothing wrong with talking about *my* father. Not the wolf. Not the alpha. Not the leader of our pack. Just plain, old, pain in my ass, *Dad.* Be real."

"So, what you're saying is not one of your daddy issues has anything to do with the strength of the pack? You be real, Reka!"

"You don't know what it's like to..." I pushed the rest of the sentence over a lump and down my throat.

"That's right. Not everyone knew their parents," Peter said. "I guess I should be pleased that you have someone that knows what they're talking about. Someone you can discuss bad father issues with."

I bit the inside of my lower lip until I tasted blood and cringed at the hurt in his eyes.

"I wish I had known mine," Peter said. "I'd trade the control issues for even a slight knowledge of who he was." Peter stuffed his hands into his pockets and stared at his feet. "Anyway, we're not talking about me or my dad. We're talking about the Alpha of our pack. Making him look bad in the community. It just doesn't feel right, that's all."

The blood in my mouth filled my senses. The pain from the bite shook me with a need for more.

Peter started walking with purpose. "You're going to get yourself into a situation that might not be any better than the one you *think* you are in now. Why don't you figure out how to tell your dad what your *real* issues are before you start giving them up to the new kid at school? That would boost the maturity you keep telling yourself—and anyone who'll listen—that you have."

I felt hurt rush my senses and settle expressively on my face. I was sure my eyes looked a lot like Peter's had minutes ago when I made remark about his father.

"Reka, we smell Otherworld all over him," Peter put his hand on my arm, "and I don't smell Down Under on him. Can you?"

I remember I had not. I'd never met a creature that didn't smell a little dark. Down Under had a unique odor. Dark, damp, a mixture of wet cement and a cave having never seen daylight. The sewer canals ran with drain water that carried discarded remains of the human world above.

I shook my head in answer to his question and lowered my eyes.

"That anomaly ought to be enough to make you slow down with this new relationship," Peter softly said, and we were walking again when he went on. "And you need to start asking him some serious questions before you spill your guts."

"It's not a relationship. Try using the word friendship. I know it's a word not often used in the pack. And no matter how much we fight; we have a relationship and friendship. However, I'm interested in getting the true meaning of simple friendship. Calastair has not even hinted he is interested in what I am other than human. If he did, I'd definitely report him. He already had one strike against him, and I checked it out. He is at Lana's. I asked him about it without hinting Otherworld. He told me his father was on a mission and couldn't take him along."

I hooded my eyes and glared at Peter. "And I sensed it wasn't a lie to cover up who or what he is or why he's here. I think it's more a punishment because of his rebellious nature."

I thought about Cal's face when I asked. It was cautious but not deceiving. "He did think a second before answering. Maybe he can't smell us either, and was just as cautious as us."

When Peter didn't answer, I added, "By the way, what are my real issues? The ones I should discuss with my father. Do you even know, Peter?"

He whipped his head around. Stormy black eyes with flashes of gold held my gaze.

"Yeah, I know," he said and put his whole body into it, arms flung, feet stomped as he walked. "You don't want me to mark you. You don't want to be my mate. I wasn't even sure you wanted to be close friends anymore, now that you found Calastair, the guy with the mysterious background."

There it was, an alpha's jealousy. I know that feeling. If Peter was getting close to a female at school I'd probably feel the same way. Peter's eyes were almost solid gold. That was anger mixed with fear. Time to back it up a bit.

"So not true," I said. "If I am going to be marked, it would be you but on my terms, equality. I want my father to know I'm not ready for any of it yet. I'm not ready to pick a mate. I'm not ready to have a litter with your eyes and my hair color. That's all, Peter. It's about timing. It isn't about you and what you mean to me."

"So, today, what do you really want? What do I mean to you?"

I let out an angry huff and headed off the path. "Evidently, you're not listening! I can't talk about this anymore." Before he could answer, I was running, and within seconds, I was on four paws and coated with black fur.

I could hear Peter going through the change behind me but was moving away from him and deeper into the woods, leaves under my paws crunched, cold and damp. I smelled the pelt of my fur, raised my maw and howled. Sounds, smells, the sun setting in the West, moon rising in the East; I was in my element ready to hunt. I ran deeper into a gradual darkness, nose in the air, eyes alert.

It took Peter minutes to turn, and only seconds for me to lose him. I could lose him, block my track, if I hit the stream ahead and swam the pond to the bog.

Peter wanted to know what Cal was and why he was here? Lana would be able to tell me, and the pack couldn't argue with that. That would be one plus of being a wolf. I wished it was the weekend. No reason to be home early on the weekend...unless I were on restriction.

I came to a slippery, sloppy halt in front of the river. I smelled a wounded deer nearby—damn hunters. At least the meat wouldn't go to waste.

Dinner first, then a trip to the boarding house.

Chapter Ten

C<u>ALASTAIR</u>

Dinner was chaos, as everything was in that house. Children screamed and threw food as Lana desperately tried to make them put it in their mouths. Credit where credit was due, she did cook pretty well. The experience was tolerable unlike the school lunch's challenge, though I did still have trouble with the whole swallowing thing.

After the children were put to bed I slunk off to my room, muscles tight and achy. I threw myself upon the scratchy sheets of the bed. *How in the father's name do Earth kids do this every day?* I wondered, and dreaded waking up tomorrow to repeat the experience. I was suddenly very eager to complete my mission, so I could return home and not have to worry about school.

I heard a rustling sound next to me and turned to see the note Lana gave me this morning. It fluttered across the room and landed on my desk. I furrowed my eyebrows and scanned the room. My eyes rested on the warped wood of the window. Must have been a draft.

I rolled over and thought about how I could explain not doing the rest of my homework. My body was content in bed, and the idea of leaving it didn't seem possible. But my mind was interrupted when I heard a buzzing sound. I turned but saw nothing.

A few seconds later, vibrating sounds returned. It seemed to be coming from my desk.

"The hell?" I stood up and walked over to it.

Buzz buzz.

I put my hand on the desk and felt the little vibrations move through it.

Buzz buzz.

I started moving papers in aggravation before I saw the note from my father start to glow. It wobbled back and forth as if trying to catch my attention. My hand rested on it and the sound stopped.

Curious, I picked it up. Reka's name disappeared to be replaced with a different message.

She suspects.

I took a deep breath as I realized this was my father's less than personal way of communicating. And I certainly didn't want to deal with it right now. But as soon as my fingers set the note down, it began buzzing and glowing again. He wasn't going away.

In a huff, I picked the note up again. "What?!"

The words again disappeared only to be replaced with the same silver ink.

She can't find out who you are.

"She doesn't know anything," I argued with the paper. "Sure, I stand out amongst the other teenagers, but just because I act a little strange doesn't automatically scream fae/angel."

It's not that easy. She isn't what you think.

I cocked my head and analyzed those words. So far, Reka hasn't seemed very different from the other kids. Well, except that I could stand her, of course. "What do you mean?"

The words disappeared, but nothing replaced them. *Oh sure, this is part of the test. Can't make this too easy, right?*

I paced the room, analyzing every moment I spent with Reka. There was something there, beneath the surface. Her behavior, her mannerisms, her solidarity, they all linked to some secret she kept buried. My tired brain couldn't put the pieces together, but it all sounded familiar.

I never liked mysteries, and despised puzzles. It was time to take a different route.

"You want me to complete this test?" I asked as crossly as possible to the note. "Fine, I get it, got to do it by myself. But you're telling me there's a risk this girl will find out who I am. That seems like a huge risk. Yet you take away my powers to help me avoid detection. So, which one of us is being reckless, Father?"

The note remained blank. But my frustration made me stand my ground. I stared at the blank paper, demanding an answer. Till, eventually, the silver words appeared.

Very well, some of your abilities will be returned to you.

I barely had time to crack a gloating smile before the room spun around me. I dropped to my knees as my head began to feel light and my skin tingled like pins and needles were poking it. I buried my face into my hands till the sensation stopped. After a few moments, I looked up to see the room no longer seemed to be moving. A few deep breaths entered my lungs. I had no idea regaining powers would be so uncomfortable.

I looked once more at the note. One last message scrolled across it slowly.

Be smart, be careful, be responsible.

"Yeah yeah. I got this."

I threw the note back on the desk. That was enough father/son bonding time for one day. I examined my body, looking for evidence of which abilities were returned to me. The first thing I checked was summoning my wings, but to my disappointment, the muscles flexed yet had no effect. The next step was to try summoning light energy to my hand, but again, no effect.

A thought crossed my mind, which brought a mischievous smile. *No; there's no way he would be cool enough to give me that.* I reached out into the air, palm flat and perpendicular to the floor. I concentrated on the air around my hand. Reality around it began to ripple, almost like my hand was cutting through a thin waterfall.

"Ha!"

I jumped though the thin barrier between realities and entered an area angels called The Gray. It was a dimension slightly out of what humans could perceive. Guarding Angels had used it since the dawn of man to watch over their assignments without being seen. I looked around me to see the world humans considered reality. It now seemed to be without color, but besides that pretty normal.

Alight, time to test this out. Lana is going to be surprised to see me jump out of thin air. I instinctively reached for the door knob just to see my hand phase through it. *That's right, different reality; this could take some getting used to.* Instead, I walked through the door and into the hall way.

By the time I reached the stairwell, I heard a knock at the front door. My mind immediately wondered if the three geeks had returned, which would have been okay if they brought more of that sweet liquid from the mountain with them.

I perched at the top of the stairs and watched Lana answer the door. I was shocked to see Reka on the other side of it, a determined expression cemented on her face.

"Reka, my dear, what are you doing here so late?" Lana asked. "It's a school night, shouldn't you be getting ready for bed?"

Reka put her hands on her hips, obviously irritated. "I know it's late. I won't be long. I just have a few questions."

From my angle I couldn't see Lana's expression, but I could picture her brow furrowing. "Alright. I'll get Cal. Just don't take too long. He's had a—"

"No. I mean, I have questions for you," Reka interrupted, staring intently at my guardian.

Lana paused, but then gestured for her to come in.

I began working my way down the stairs. My mind raced at why Reka would be here, asking my caregiver questions. I thought once again of my father's letter. 'She suspects,' he said. Perhaps he wasn't being over cautious. But last I saw her she was smiling. What could have happened since? I realized a little pang of disappointment coursed through me at the thought of her questioning Lana instead of bringing her questions to me. I had thought I earned her trust. Why wasn't she asking to see me?

"I'm sorry the place is such a mess," Lana said, shuffling out of place couch cushions. "It can get crazy around here."

"It's fine. I'm used to it." Reka looked around the room as Lana straightened. She settled on a picture on the wall. It had a group of children playing on the lawn.

I leaned in to get a better look. When I did, Reka snapped her head to look right at me.

I jumped back.

Her eyes seemed to follow me. *No way! She can't see me while I'm in The Gray!* I shifted to the left, then the right. Her eyes followed but were always a second behind.

"What's wrong, dear?" Lana asked.

"I just...no, never mind." She casted one last curious glance in my direction then sat across from Lana on the couch.

My nerves were rattled. How could she possibly have sensed me? She wasn't what I thought indeed. No human could have known I was there.

"So, what can I help you with?" Lana asked politely as she folded her hands on her lap.

Reka crossed her arms and leaned back. "I just wanted to know about Cal. We spent a lot of time together today. Kind of strange how he was in every one of my classes."

"I'm sure he's not the only one. As I recall, he's signed up for quite a few general Ed classes."

Reka nodded. "Fair enough. But he's not quite...normal, is he?"

"What's normal, dear?" Lana smiled. "I would say he is a bit of a fish out of water, still getting used to a new town and all."

Reka's eyes shot daggers. "It's more than that, though, isn't it?"

Lana's smile faded. "I don't follow you."

Even in The Gray, I could see Reka's cheeks darken.

"Don't do that. I'm not some stupid little brat!" She leaned forward. "This house reeks of Otherworld. It's not a secret. Why everyone from Down Under tip toes around discussion of this place is beyond me. Frankly, I don't care. But Cal has some interest in me, and it's causing problems. I just want to know what they are, so I can get certain people off my back."

My attention shifted from Reka, to Lana, and back. I had to stop this. I trusted Lana not to tell my secret, but only bad things could come from this. Suspicion as to why Lana wouldn't tell her the truth, caution around everything I did and said. I couldn't have her questioning my intentions.

My mind raced to find an answer when the room started spinning again. Just like before, I dropped to the floor. I could feel my skin begin to tingle. I could feel my footing in The Gray give way. *Not now, not now!*

I slammed my eyes shut to keep from getting too woozy. The sensation began to pass, and I could automatically feel my new abilities kick in. Angels had a sixth sense to feel the life force around them. I could feel the energy given off by the twins upstairs in their room. I could sense what they actually were. Imps! That made sense. I also could feel some of the other's life force. This house was a collection of lost children from heaven and from hell.

My attention shifted quickly to Reka. I could hear her heart beat and sense struggle within it. Something loomed deep down, scratching, clawing to get out. A curse housed deep inside, waiting to be released. It was something I'd felt before.

My eyes snapped open. The world was no longer spinning, but it also had returned to color. I had lost my grasp on The Gray and was spat back out into the human world. I saw Lana and Reka staring at me, confusion and surprise frozen on their faces.

I studied Reka as I realized what my father had meant. "You're a werewolf?!"

Chapter Eleven

R^{EKA} "You are not human either, Calastair!" Popped out of my mouth, and it was too late to take back. But I was pleasantly surprised to watch Cal's face filled with amazement, transition as his mouth snapped shut and his eyes became smaller under a furrowed brow.

"Who told you I'm a werewolf?"

My mouth watered. The air in the house was heavy with smells of dinner, hamburgers and french-fries.

"I just figured it out," Cal said. "You didn't feel as human as the rest of the kids at school."

I held his gaze and waited while I filtered other odors hanging on to things in the house: lavender, bleach, sandalwood, candle wax, and a lemony, wood oil. They mingled with the heady scents of Otherworld creatures left on the material of couch cushions and throw pillows. French dormer windows running the wall beside the front door were slightly open letting fall smells ride a crisp, fall breeze. Day and night were changing shifts, and this home was warm and welcoming.

Cal sighed. "I know you felt me while I was in The Gray, Reka, even though you couldn't see me. That isn't all together human either."

"The Gray?" I asked. *Like, what the crap is The Gray?* I'd never heard the expression. "Is it like a portal or rift?" When he looked at me, forehead furrowed, eyes all squinty, I added, "An opening to another realm. Kind of like a time warp or passage to another world or planet or something. Did you ever watch *Dr. Who*?"

His chest rose and fell while his lips tensed. I stole a glance at Lana, but she was intently watching Cal.

"Down Under," I said, "some species buy or barter for coins to get from one place to another. Is 'The Gray' like that?"

"Uh, sort of," Cal said. "But I didn't pay passage."

He stared at me.

I raised an eyebrow.

"And, well, here on Earth The Gray is more like a cloak to make me invisible. It doesn't take me anywhere, per say."

His gaze fell to my jaw. I was grinding my teeth.

"The Gray is a part of where I am from," he said.

Crap, crap, and triple crap! He IS a space alien!

Our heads jerked up with the pitter-patter of tiny feet and loud, squealy giggles.

"Alright, you two," Lana said. "It's a school night. You can trade superpower information tomorrow. I don't want the others coming down to see what the commotion is about."

"Yeah. That's probably a good idea," Cal said, and his body relaxed. "The twins were on the floor in the hall playing a game with star shaped metal pieces and a small rubber ball." His eyes darted from Lana, to me, and back again. "They couldn't see me, so they probably still think I'm in my room studying."

"I need to ask you a couple of questions *tonight*, Cal. Privately." I nodded at Lana. "Do you think I could talk to him on the porch for a sec?"

I really wanted to hear more about that Gray place, but most of all, I needed to nail down where he was from and how he guessed about me. I needed an explanation for my father and Peter. Cal knew I was a werewolf, and at the very least, was pretty darn sure Peter and my father were shifters as well. I'd put them in jeopardy. That would be something Dad would need to rectify.

I didn't want to move again. We'd moved the pack three times since I was born. And, luckily, all we left behind was wonder. Anonymity was sacred among all Down Under. The Otherworld council would step in if this got out of hand like when Mom died. A pack member, in a panic, took Mom to a local hospital where she died giving birth to me and my sister. The coroner was baffled, and the council had some clean up. I was unaware of that mess until I was fourteen.

"I don't think going outside at this hour is a good idea," Lana said. "It's late and—"

"But it's important!" I whipped my lips from pouty to angry and blinked the disappointment from my eyes. "Look, I came here because I have time restraints. I need information tonight for—"

"Sweetheart, at your age, everything is important, and there is always a deadline," Lana said. "Is it a situation that threatens either of your lives tonight or tomorrow?"

"Well, no. But—"

"Reka." Lana looked sympathetic but unyielding. "Calastair's father left him in my care with a strict list of instructions. Besides taking my guardianship seriously, my house is run by a schedule and rules. If I break rules for one, I have to do the same for others." She curled her lower lip and blew a breath out her nose. "I'm sorry. Tomorrow will have to be soon enough. I'm sure your father is home waiting for you, Reka. Does he know where you are?"

Okay, so having her call my father is absolutely NOT a good idea, and besides that, I don't want to burn any bridges. I may need Lana if I leave the pack.

"Dad knew I was out on the hunt with Peter. Full moon and all," I felt myself blush, "but I'm sure Peter and the others are back at the house by now. You're right. I should get home."

My quick response in her favor visibly knocked Cal's tension down a notch, and I realized the degree of Lana's determination after her shoulders relaxed and she smiled. Opening a dialogue tomorrow at school would probably be wiser anyway. And the pack meeting wasn't until tomorrow tonight anyway.

"Sorry I'm being such a drama queen," I mumbled to Cal. "You want to meet in the common area before school tomorrow?"

"Sure." Cal smiled. "You bring your questions and I'll bring mine. I'm eager to find out what that time restraint thing is all about."

Crap! I'm an idiot! Now I have to share more of me with him. What the heck have I done? "Will do." *Did I just squawk? I sounded like a chicken. Is he smiling? Ugh!*

Lana bit her lower lip, and then turned to Cal. She swung her arm toward the landing where he had appeared a few minutes ago. "Off with you, mister; shower, homework, and lights out by ten."

"Will do," Cal said, and he waved at me. "Goodnight, Reka."

He didn't turn back and walked out of the living room as much a human as I did. I momentarily wondered if 'the twins' were still in the hall playing *Jacks*—another reason an alien sounded right for Cal; he had no clue. Who didn't know a game of *Jacks* when they saw it? Whatever planet Cal was from, they sure didn't do their due diligence before beaming him down. Now that I thought about it, there were a lot of weird things about Cal that should have clued me that this was his first time on earth. Hey, that bit of information I could take to my father and Peter if they asked tonight. Alien works.

Ten minutes later, I was running through the woods on four paws headed for home, my senses alive. The night air that carried a damp chill, and the chatter of nature as it settled in, was tainted by my rambling mind full of questions. Should I really tell my father or Peter that I was pretty darn sure Cal was an extraterrestrial creature? That he knew I was a shifter? And that tomorrow I was going to find out what planet he was from and why he was here?

If I did, I would have to tell them I didn't know how I knew, or how he found out about the werewolf thing. If I told the truth, they wouldn't believe it. If I lied, they'd only find out and never trust me for sure. It was all so confusing. Why did I have to answer to them anyway? I was almost an adult! This was bull! No matter what I decided, one thing was for sure, I would not tell either of them I was about to spill my guts in the morning.

It was time I had a real friend outside the pack even if part of me knew telling them was the right thing to do. But I was tired of letting the pack dominate my decisions. Tired of having to bone up but remain forever lesser-than just because I was a girl. It wasn't right. Besides, what harm was there in sharing a bit more of me now? Calastair already knew I was a werewolf.

And besides that, couldn't his alien buddies find out everything about me if he really was extraterrestrial?

Wait!

If?

Come on! I'm a werewolf! I've met vampires and fairies, trolls and a poltergeist, witches and sorcerers, ghosts, and a demon named Harold. Aliens were not a big stretch.

The wolf in me, on autopilot, scrambled over and around a nettle patch as my human half wondered what aliens really looked and smelled like. Cal had an unusual scent, and...

Ohmigod, would he have a big head and hollow black eyes without his guise? Was his space ship hidden in the woods outside town? What if he had half the city hypnotized? Aliens could do that. Were there more of them here? Was he going to go all *Invasion of the Body Snatchers* on us? Oh, man!

Maybe I watched too many horror movies.

I jumped a fallen log, kicked up a pile of leaves and twigs on the other side, and as I scampered through the dark night, and took huge gulps of air through an open maw, tongue hung out the side. Boy, I loved the woods. And nothing was more exuberating than a night run.

Should I tell Peter? I leapt over a depression on the ground—*should I tell Dad?*—and hit the dirt path to the cabin. Jade popped into my mind ana quickly faded. He was not trustworthy. But he sure was cute.

I smelled smoke from the woodstove that heated the log cabin. Our home was three stories tall, if you didn't count the locked rooms below the half-buried level under the living room and kitchen. I loved the house; the communal living, too. There was always someone to talk to.

Maybe that was the answer. I could talk to Boggy or Raz. Either would listen and keep it between us if I made them promise. Bogdan, Boggy for short, was kind and understanding. He also treated female wolves equal, and never underestimated a woman's strength. He was protective of all pack members equally, and openly gave everyone the same respect.

I came to a trot as I neared the path because I knew I should change, but the night was so much more in wolf form. I stopped, fell on to my back, and moved my head and butt in different directions to scratch my back on the earth. I'd smell the outdoors on me until I showered.

When I stood, I shook from maw to tail and blew a snorted huff.

I looked at the lit cabin and saw Raz pass by the living room window. He was big, scary, easy to anger, quick to defend, but a big teddy bear with me. In wolf form, Raz was powerful, with a deep threatening bark and a deadly growl. He was as scary as a black bear. But he let me hug him and scratch his head, tail wagging. He often slept on the floor by my sister's bed in wolf form. Dedicated to defending the weakest of the pack first.

When defending the pack, Raz fought women and men alike without giving gender, or the outcome, second thought. He was the only member to tell me outright I could lead the pack if Dad died. He taught me to fight and told me my ability to shift in seconds could get me there. It took minutes for most to shift. It only took me seconds. That, he said, was a better weapon than a knife or gun in battle.

But he also said we had to work on control if I wanted to last as a pack leader. I got that. I mean, I cut myself. And I had an uncontrollable nature. I knew I had issues. But doesn't everyone?

I loved Raz dearly, and never felt uncomfortable telling him anything, because he always called me out if I was being stupid. Boggy was more like an older brother. He would listen and tell me gently if he thought I was wrong. Not Raz. He was loud, obnoxious, and used sentences like: "Do you want to die? Have you taken another stupid-pill today? Do I need to lock you in one of the rooms under the house until you come to your senses?" He made me laugh. My snarky answers made him laugh, too.

Sprinting down the rest of the path, the house yards away, I phased into a human and climbed the steps to the front door, fully clothed. It always amazed me the way my clothes turned to fur or back to clothing as I shifted. That was something fiction writers were not aware of. Good thing, I guess.

Feeling comfortable with my decision to keep this from my father and Peter tonight and talk to Raz or Boggy before school tomorrow, I entered the house with a smile lifting my cheeks.

Until I saw Dad.

He sat in a big leather chair by the fireplace in the living room. His eyes caught the flames and flashed gold. A growl hummed deep in his throat. The house was exceptionally quiet for eight o'clock.

"Sit down," he said in a gravelly voice. "We need to talk."

Crap. This was so not good.

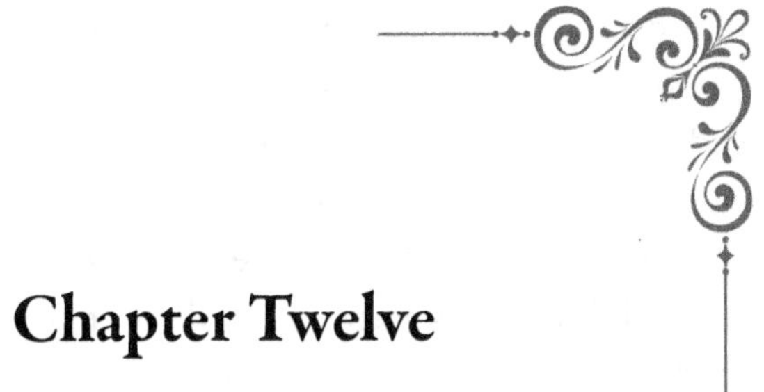

Chapter Twelve

CALASTAIR

I laid on my bed, staring at the stippled ceiling. My clock read 11:00, and I was given to believe that was late. I knew Lana wanted me to be asleep by now, but since I'd never slept before, I didn't know how to start. My bed creaked with every turn, its lumpy mattress refusing to let me find comfort.

I thought back to Reka's visit, about how I appeared out of The Gray like that. Now she knew I was not a regular human. And how stupid I had been to blurt out she was a werewolf, and that I wasn't from this Earth? I failed on every level.

I rested the back of my hand against my forehead. "Damnit!" I shouted in disgust. Why did she come here anyway? To ask Lana about me. Why was she so curious? Had I acted that strange at school? Or was there another reason? I guess that was something I should add to the list to ask her tomorrow.

In some ways, it was comforting to know Reka was a werewolf. It'd be easier to relate to her now, us both being non-humans. She had to feel out casted from the people around her, alone in a crowded room. I certainly knew a thing or two about that.

But it was also going to make things harder. I didn't know a ton about werewolves, but I knew they were pack oriented, loyal to each other and few others. That probably explained Peter's reaction toward me. I could only assume the rest of the pack would feel similarly. They could interfere with everything I was trying to do. And what if to accomplish my mission Reka would need to side with me over her pack? Was that even possible?

I sat up on the side of the bed, letting my bare feet rest on the cold wood floor. My fingers rustled my copper hair in frustration. On the desk was my father's letter. I snatched it.

"A freaking werewolf?!" I asked the paper.

And to my surprise, words immediately appeared.

Werewolves didn't ask for this curse; heaven is not blind to them.

I sighed. He was missing the point again. "I know that. It's just, it's my first time on guardian duty. Couldn't ya have started me on someone a little more...normal?"

This isn't supposed to be easy, Cal. It's a trial.
An opportunity to show your qualities.

A trial by fire was more like it. I tapped the letter against my arm as I paced the room. "Ya know, I was thinking, since she is a werewolf, it really wouldn't hurt that much to tell her who I am. We're both considered 'supernatural' by these humans, so—"

The paper vibrated and started to glow as the letters appeared.

DO NOT tell her!

I expected my father would need to be talked into the idea, but the intensity of his answer surprised me. "Why not?"

There are checks and balances to consider.
If it became known Guardian Angels exist, there could be chaos.

"I'm not talking about announcing it to the whole world, just this one girl."

No, Calastair! I gave you some powers back in an effort to hide you, not expose us.

It's bad enough she knows what she knows.

There it was. I knew it would come up eventually. "That wasn't my fault. The power transfer distracted me. I lost control of The Gray and slipped out."

I realize that.

There was a delay with the transfer and the timing was unfortunate.

But you can't compound one mistake with another.

"But—"

Stay safe, Calastair. Stay hidden.

The note faded. I was tempted to try and coerce more discussion, but figured it was pointless. I set the note down. My muscles felt weaker.

I laid back down on the bed. My mind wandered to tomorrow's conversation. What was I going to tell Reka? Surely her first question was going to be what kind of creature I was. Maybe there was another being out there with similar powers. After all, all she saw was me come out of The Gray.

I closed my eyes and let my mind search itself, but no answers came. Even the simpler thoughts seemed blocked by fatigue. But even if I could think of something, I wasn't sure I wanted to lie to Reka. If she caught me, any trust I gained with her would be gone.

I laid there for a few more minutes, trying to come up with an answer. Before I knew it, the energy in my body seemed to leave me. My mind wandered to places and events far away, and my muscles no longer responded to command. Soon, I lost consciousness.

Chapter Thirteen

REKA

I stood in the living room and stared at my father. "I was in a great mood until I walked in that door." He looked upset. "Clearly you're freaking about something...again. I'm tired, Dad. Can we do this tomorrow?"

He didn't say a word, and as I listened to his chest rumble, watched his jaw tighten, I became aware of how quiet the house was beyond the crackling fire and my father's angry animal noises. Our house was never silent, not even in the middle of the night. I looked around, nose in the air. And I didn't even scent Buddy. He always greeted me. Not tonight. Something was wrong.

"What happened?" I asked, tension building. Maybe this wasn't about me. "Where is everyone?"

"Raz took them to the bowling alley for pizza." His words came out authoritative, not concerned. "I asked him to hang out until I called."

Okay, so this was definitely about me. I felt relieved, but so not in the mood for one of my father's 'talks', tonight. "Even Buddy?" I asked, stalling the inevitable.

"Yes," my father said curtly, and pointed to the chair facing him from the other side of the fireplace. "There will be no interruptions, Reka."

This was so not good. I opened my mouth but shut it again. I'd never seen him this angry.

"Sit down!"

"Look—"

"Now!" Dad bolted up from the chair, hands balled at his hips. "Unless you want me to assist you."

I dropped my bookbag by the chair and sat. The heat from the fire warmed my legs immediately. My wolf wanted to curl up on the rug in front of the hearth , back to the fire.

"You haven't listened to me with respect since you turned fifteen. Tonight, I'm not asking for respect, but I'm damn sure ordering you to listen. I've had quite enough of your belligerent disposition. I warn you. I will not tolerate it tonight."

My wolf roiled inside. I clamped my teeth down, diverted my eyes, and the alpha in me thought about challenging him. Right here. Right now. Instead, I concentrated on my breathing. But if I didn't calm down, I was going to go all rabid on him.

As my father sat, I stole a look. His eyes were hard, lined in wolf gold, but his forehead wrinkled with concern. He caught me watching him, and the wolf gold widened. I held my ground even though I should lower my eyes. It was not respectful or smart. Especially when he was in alpha mode.

Fighting the change, I asked, "What happened?"

Another no-no. I was still a minor, and technically it was not only my father demanding attention but the pack leader. He would severely punish anyone else acting this way. And it's not often controllable. A wolf is a wild animal. Offspring were not considered anything more than a member, and all valued equally by what they could do to strengthen the pack. So, the wolf instinctually wanted to protect me but wouldn't think twice about destroying me if I endangered his members.

"Do you know three students by the names of Johnathan, Daniel, and Tiffany?"

I stiffened, sat back in the chair, blew out a slow breath through my nose, crossed my ankles, and forced myself to relax. "Vaguely. They're in a couple of my classes. Why?"

"They were at Lana's rooming house today, boldly speaking on the front porch with a border."

I swallowed hard, forced a smile, and prayed this wasn't about Cal. "Really? Were you watching the house?"

"No. I've had David following them on all four since Johnathan turned eighteen. They're becoming more aggressive in their queries about us, and Lana's foster home. Lately, all three have made public they're sure our town is laden with supernatural creatures."

"Oh," I said. My heart raced. "Peter and I don't hang with any of them."

"That's not entirely true," my father said. "Is it?"

"It damn sure is." I was angry now. "We do not encourage, acknowledge, or give them more than an occasional glance like the rest of the kids in town."

"You've been seen with a redheaded boy several times this week. And he just happened to be the one visited by them at Lana's. Since he immediately took up with the three sleuths after moving into the boarding house, it disturbed the council enough to look into him." He paused and studied me while I almost died.

"They were unable to find anything that ties the anomaly to the humans or Otherworld creatures. Most of all, Lana believes the boy in her charge is as innocent as he is naïve, and that Johnathan and the others are using him. As per the rules of ethics, the council was unable to ask his breed or nature. But Lana did say he was as Otherworld as all of her borders."

Dad lifted his nose to the air and then seemed to relax a bit. He smelled my rising fear. "None the less, there are quite a few of us on alert."

I sucked in a breath. My father sharpened his stare and outwardly studied me. I wish he'd just spit out why. The suspense was killing me.

"I know you're talking about Cal." My voice was snappy but weak.

"Yes," Dad said. "Calastair."

I attempted to settle back in the chair. Wolves were good at scenting weakness—my father was a master. I had to get control of myself.

"Before I ask for further explanation," Dad said, "I'll give you the same respect I would give another pack member of your caliber and tell you why I'm asking. I demand your respect in return. Do not repeat our conversation to anyone, including Peter. Do you understand?"

I felt relieved and shook my head up and down like a ten-year-old asked to go to Dairy Dip.

"Good, because if the council believes you are part of this, it will not be me who reprimands you or sets punishment. In fact, I will immediately escort you Down Under without recourse."

My father was on the panel of twelve Otherworld creatures; a council that upheld order and anonymity above ground in the upper state, Michigan tri-county community. They were also sworn to protect humans from us.

I was nervous. What if Cal was part of some conspiracy with the geeks to out the town? What if Lana didn't even know? *I don't really believe that, do I?* I sat tall and said nothing.

Elbow on the arm of his chair, Dad leaned sideways and placed a balled hand against his mouth as he studied me through long lashes. I counted twelve beats of my heart before Dad said anything.

"The council is meeting right now to decide if I should visit Castifyn's coven in Tuskin."

He let that sink in a second before it hit me.

Ohmigod, they were going to do a mind wipe! It's a prerequisite to stronger defense tactics. Three immortals act as exorcists. But instead of chasing away demons, they cleanse the offenders' minds of knowledge, understanding, and concern toward anything involving the world Down Under and us. It wasn't done often; in fact, the last time was before I was born. Papo and David talked about Dad and Raz being part of that one. I made a mental note to ask Raz about it. I thought of asking Dad if I could attend and quickly thought better of it.

"Now tell me," Dad said. "What do you know of these three students, and can you connect them to your new friend, Calastair?"

And there it was. Almost relief. He wanted my help.

"They're definitely a little too curious about Peter and me. But I chalked that up to us being a tad weirder than the rest of the kids at school. And I don't for one-minute think Calastair is part of any plan to out us. In fact, he seems immature as far as human ways. It's almost humorous." Why was I grinding my teeth? "How many of the other pack members know about the mind melt?"

"Raz and Papo," Dad answered. "Most of the others are aware the three teens have had a special interest in our pack and Lana's boarding house for a few years. While the kids were too young to be taken seriously or to leave town with any pertinent information, they were not a threat. However, they're no longer just a thorn in our sides.

"They have cell phones with cameras, and Johnathan just received an automobile for his eighteenth birthday. His ability to get around will no longer restricted.

"Tiffany no longer pretends she has a crush on Peter while she attempts to pry, and Daniel has become an avid paranormal reader and has turned into a first-rate blabbermouth.

"Look at their direct and fearless attempt to get information out of Cal, simply because you are showing him attention."

"This is cracked," I said, still feeling tense, but not threatened. At least Dad hadn't forbidden me from talking with Cal. "I'm so tired of this crap. I wish the whole world knew we were here. Why should we hide?"

"It is what it is, Reka. We are what we are and would seem a huge threat to humans should they find out. Lighten up. It's a good thing this new friend of yours is not human. You can warn him about them and enlighten him about our intentions. Tell Calastair of Johnathan, Tiffany, and Daniel's intent to drag us out into the open. Do this, even if Lana beats you to it, and especially if you wish to remain friends with Calastair."

I couldn't breathe. Holy crap, this was big. But something told me not to make it so. "I'll warn Cal tomorrow. I can't call him tonight. I don't think he even owns a cell phone, never mind how to use it. Besides, it's lights out early on school nights at Lana's."

"How refreshing," Dad said.

"What? The cell phone or lights out?"

"Both." He smiled, and added, "So, do you have any idea what kind of creature this Calastair character is?"

Crap.

"Not exactly," I said.

"Excuse me?"

"Well, Cal is a new friend, and I didn't want—"

"We don't make friends without observing, sensing, and then questioning if we believe they're Otherworld like us."

"I do." Who was I kidding? I have never made friends outside the pack.

"No. You do not. It's too dangerous. And this is a perfect example."

My father was back, the gold rings around his irises were faded, and there was a curve to his lips, but he was swift to anger, so I smiled back.

"I know what it's like to be young," he said. "To need to explore and expand your world, but it's dangerous if you are lax about pack rules, Reka. Not just for you, but for all of us." He puffed a sigh. "Because Lana vouched for your new friend, I'm not going to forbid you to speak to him. But the minute you prove to be lax in your understanding of how much you need to use good judgement with this new relationship, I'll nip it quickly. Clear?"

"Dad, it's the twenty-first century. I know you're old, set in your ways, but it's time for a change. I refuse to be governed by ancient rules. I should be able to make Otherworld friends just like you have. You're going to knock on the coffins of a vampire coven without concern. You serve on a council comprised of fifteen Otherworld creatures, and Lana babysits a houseful of them. Making friends can be an asset, especially if they know what we are and accept it."

My father bent forward in his chair, and one elbow on his knee, index finger waging, he sternly said, "Are you telling me this Calastair guy—looks can be deceiving with underworld creatures by the way—knows what you are? And you have no idea what he is?"

Double crap. "Pretty much. Cal guessed tonight at Lana's after I witnessed him appear from nowhere."

"You went to Lana's tonight?" His voice was guttural. "Even knowing it's strictly forbidden by me, the council, and Lana because it could alert human residents of possible connections?"

Triple crap.

"It's a stupid rule." *What the heck am I doing*? "Us staying away from each other attracts unwanted attention, and it's probably why the Geek Squad is watching Lana's house and interested in our pack."

"You knew they were watching the property and didn't tell anyone?"

I had an answer for that one. "No, not until Cal told me at school today. He said Johnathan told him a bunch of us live in the woods in a big log cabin. And I was going to tell Peter that tonight, but he was a crab after school because you keep riding him to bite my neck and mark me. So, I was upset with him, and that's why I went to talk to Lana about Cal. I wanted to be friends and thought Lana might tell me what Cal was because Peter and I smelled he was not human."

"And how did that work for you?" Dad asked angrily.

I sighed and averted my eyes. "Not well."

I couldn't believe I'd spent time trying to keep this information from him while arguing with Peter and threatening him if he said anything. And then, like an idiot, I blurted the whole thing out.

"Peter will mark you after the meeting if I have to hold you down for him to do so."

"Like hell he will!" I shouted and instinctively searched for Buddy who always came to my defense. Not tonight. "I'm not eighteen yet. I don't have to submit."

"You need the protection of other packs as well as ours. And it's about time you realize who you are and what your place is. If you need time to think about it, I can put you in one of the basement rooms until you turn eighteen. What will it be?"

It looked like I might end up spending more than a couple of days locked up. But I wasn't going to tell my father that until after tomorrow's talk with Cal.

"Fine!" I shouted. "I'll think about it. And if I do let him it's only because I know Peter won't hold me to a union I don't want to be in. But it's still not right."

"Good. I'll give Raz a call and let him know we are finished here. Now, up to your bedroom with you." My father stood, tugged his shirt into place, and leveled his gaze on me. He shook a finger in my direction. "Our conversation tonight does not give you a green light to do anything that you know goes against pack rules. Don't make me do something I wish not to do, Reka. I need to go Down Under and will likely have to go to Castifyn's coven afterward. I'll check with Raz in an hour to be sure your homework is complete, and you're tucked in with Buddy."

I snagged my bookbag by the chair and slung it over my shoulder, and without looking back, took the stairs to my room two at a time. I was going to have my meeting with Cal in the morning because, right now, he was the only unbiased friend I had. I didn't care what happened next. I was not letting Peter bite me after the meeting, no matter the outcome.

IT WAS A CRISP AND windy morning with brightly colored leaves raining down on me as I took a path through the woods to school. I popped out one street north of the high school, cut through a graveyard and more woods southeast of the school. I had no idea how much of the conversation with Dad I was going to lay on Cal, other than warning him the geeks really screwed up by knocking on Lana's door. Finding out some basics about Cal was top priority, though.

I came out of the woods behind the junior high parking lot and felt vulnerable as I zig-zagged around busses and cars letting students off in front of the entrance. The high school was behind the junior high. I had to jog around the building and past the auditorium to get to the common area between the two levels of education. That was where Cal was waiting.

I spotted him the minute I entered the commons. The area was littered with students standing in groups or sitting on the grass. Cal sat alone on a cement bench under a large maple on the other side of the court. He was face down inside a book, a beacon of carrot-red hair tossed by the wind.

He didn't look up when I approached. Odd. The wind was at my back. I would have got a scent. The soap I bathed with if nothing else.

Cal had a smell all his own. It was air after a light rain in the summer—soft and safe—with an under scent of burnt umber and sage—earthy and dark but not always safe. It really threw me off. I couldn't pin it down. It was a shame Lana was forbidden to give Dad even a piece of clothing to try to identify Cal, but the council also protected us from one another as well the humans. I didn't have time to dwell on that because a piece of paper got away from Cal. He jumped up to catch it but caught sight of me and missed. It blew over his head and across the grass behind him.

"Was there something important on that piece of paper?" I asked, pointing at it. The wind flattened it against a trashcan about fifteen feet away.

Cal turned to look. "No. Nothing, actually. I was using it as a bookmark. But I should probably still grab it. After all, I wouldn't want a strike against me for littering."

We had ten minutes to get to our first class. "Can you just leave it a second?" Peter would be looking for me at our lockers by now and I wanted to get on with this.

"Sure," Cal answered and sat down beside me on the bench.

"Have you been here like forever?" I asked.

Cal smiled, and my stomach fluttered. "Are you asking me if I'm immortal? Or are you concerned you made me wait too long?"

Every time he opened his mouth his choice of words forced a giggle up my throat and I immediately swallowed. "Yeah. I'll go with the immortal thing since you opened that door."

He chuckled. "My world is forever immortal, but there are worse deaths than a natural death like humans experience on this planet."

There he goes with the planet thing again. "So, you are an alien?"

"I fell asleep wondering if I could trust you with information my father specifically asked me to keep to myself while on earth," Cal said. "I can't take his request lightly. He's a human breath away from snatching me back if I do."

"And?" The paper was still flat against the trashcan. And I couldn't take my eyes off it.

"And do I trust you?"

I nodded.

"I will tell you my mother was fae because she's no longer alive. I never knew her, but my father speaks of her often. He is immortal. I don't think he would object to my telling you this. As to whether or not he's an alien...I guess that depends on what your definition of an alien is."

What an alien thing to say. I knew it! Why was everything about aliens so hush-hush? It made me nuts.

"Why are you here? Why isn't there anyone who can watch over you on your own planet? And how long are you staying at Lana's?"

"Whoa, girl. Slow down," Cal said. "You know what I am. I know what you are. Quid pro quo. My turn, right?"

Ugh! I so wanted to know everything before the first bell. "Fine. Your turn, but we may want to head toward our lockers pretty soon."

Cal rolled his eyes, shoved the book he was reading into a satchel at his feet, and then jogged off to retrieve the paper. It gave me an opportunity to notice others watching us. They diverted their gaze as my eyes searched them out.

Cal came bouncing back, paper in hand. "Are werewolves immortal?" he asked.

I hefted my backpack higher on my shoulder. "Before I answer, did Lana say anything to you this morning?"

"About last night?"

We stood looking at each other. Cal looked tense.

"No. About Johnathan, Tiffany, and Daniel?"

"Yes. And Lana said you might mention it as well because your father was going to talk to you last night." He raked a hand through his disorderly red hair. "I hope he wasn't too hard on you. Lana said you were not supposed to visit the boarding house."

"We can get to that later during dance class, but for now, maybe you should distance yourself from them, or at least be cautious of what you say. The council freaks me out sometimes. I try not to cross them."

"Yeah, I hear your father is on the panel. I'm not going to push them away. I believe it wise to keep an eye on your enemies. Don't you?"

"Yeah, well, let's get back to us while we have a minute." I nudged him and pointed at his books on the bench. "The whole freaking school is watching us. Can't I do anything without... Never mind. In answer to your question about mortality. No, but we have pretty long lives," I said softly. "My dad looks thirtyish, but they had me in their mid-forties." I studied the crowd while he processed that, then said, "My turn. Why are you here?"

"My father is on...uh...a job-related mission," Cal said, his hand over his mouth, eyes darting around. "And it would not have benefitted either of us if I tagged along."

"You are definitely not accustomed to the word stealth, are you? Jeez, just relax and act normal, will ya." I nodded at the books and then toward a sidewalk as noisy kids began to head to different entrances.

Cal grabbed the notepad and Algebra book and reached down to tuck them into the leather satchel. "Since I'd already answered this question the day we met, I'll give you another try." He moved slowly and tried not to stare at students walking by even though they slowed down as they passed.

"How long are you staying?" I asked and felt a twang of regret because if Cal said weeks or even months, it would make me count the days and dwell on it. I hadn't realized how upset I'd be if we had only a few weeks or something. I felt good when I was around him. No pack. Just two Otherworld kids at school. And lately, thoughts of him consumed me. My stomach felt hollow, and I pushed it away, reminding myself I'd climbed out the bedroom window and missed breakfast to dodge Dad.

"I'm not sure," Cal said, and frown lines formed over his eyebrows. "Whenever the...uh, that is, when Dad's business is complete." He leaned into my ear, and I got goosebumps when he whispered, "Time moves slower where I'm from. So—"

"Any idea? Just toss something out there?" I almost shouted. Several students couldn't hold back a giggle, and it pissed me off.

Why was I obsessed with when he was leaving, anyway? I should have been asking him about fae magic, or get more information on his father, or if he had ever been Down Under, and there was the way he ate. He acted like he'd never eaten macaroni and cheese or drank bottled beverages. Every kid has had both, like forever. What was up with that?

"I believe it's my turn," Cal was stiffly saying. He adjusted the bookbag slung it over his shoulder. "Did you tell your father about me?" he asked.

A knot formed in my empty gut.

"Yes." I grabbed a handful of the sweater on his shoulder, dragged him down to my level, and hissed in his ear, "So do you have any more of your mother's magic than jumping in and out of The Gray?"

Cal straightened up. "Hold on," he said, pausing a few feet from the door to the hall that held our lockers. "Can you please expand on my question beyond a 'yes'?"

Crap. "Okay, so that's going to take a few minutes to answer."

"No problem," he said as he opened the door for me and doubled the noise and students moving around us. "I'm a good listener."

Double crap!

Chapter Fourteen

CALASTAIR
I listened to Reka talk about her conversation with her father. The information she gave him about me seemed relatively harmless. It was uncomfortable having her father keeping eyes on my activities, but it made me feel better knowing I wasn't his main concern. Although, I was surprised to hear the three geeks were.

"Wow, your father had a big wig out over John, Tiffany, and Daniel?" I laughed. "Those three are persistent, maybe bordering on annoying sometimes, but not dangerous."

"Oh please. You know the concerns of outsiders learning about us. Especially kids in this school. There're dumb ass rumors bouncing around here every day. Those three find out, everyone finds out."

"Huh, I hadn't thought of that." She made a good point. "But there's so much mindless gossip around here. I doubt anyone would take them too seriously."

"Yeah, maybe," Reka shrugged. "The council has watched them for a while now, but with this new attention they've given you—walking right up to Lana's and knocking on the door—it's made them nervous. Guess it doesn't matter too much if the council does the mind wipe on them. Anyway, I have a couple of questions about The Gray—"

"Wait, what?!" I said too loudly. Other students turned toward us with interest. I gave them a somewhat nervous smile, trying to play like things were alright before pushing Reka away from the door and prying ears. "Did you say the council was going to do a mind wipe on those three?!" My lowered tone made the question come out in more of a hiss.

Reka frowned. "It's my turn, Cal."

"This is important, Reka. Is the council using magic for memory manipulation?"

She examined my face. I could tell her eyes were searching, confused over my sudden eruption. "No. Vampires. It's not something they usually do, if that's what you're worried about, but it's more of a last-ditch action. They actually wipe out everything that has to do with us being anything other human. Whatever they got to do to remain hidden, ya know."

That didn't comfort me. Memory manipulation was very tricky magic. One slip up could mean the difference between erasing a single memory, or everything that makes them who they are. Worse yet, it was because of me the three were drawing the council's attention. If anything happened to them, it'd be my fault. One of the first rules of being a Guardian Angel was to avoid altering the paths of anyone besides their ward. I couldn't risk any harm coming to them.

"Reka, you need to tell me everything you know about the council, and everything you know about the spell the vampires use."

"When did this turn into an interrogation?" she asked, taking a step back and crossing her arms.

"I'm sorry. It's just...this is important, and dangerous. I can't let the council do anything that could harm those three."

Reka threw her hands up. "Cal, I'm not even supposed to tell you any of this, now suddenly you want to take on the council?! You know how much trouble I could get into if anyone found out what I've told you?"

Great. I hadn't thought of that. I started playing out scenarios in my head. How could I interfere with the council's plans without endangering her? The situation was a lot more complicated than I thought.

The school bell rang, signaling we had five minutes left before class started.

Reka grabbed my arm. "Crap, we got to go. We'll talk about this after class."

MY MIND WAS TOO DISTRACTED by thoughts of the council to focus on the class lecture. The math teacher seemed aware and called on me repeatedly to answer questions on the board. By the end I just shouted out random numbers, not concerned if they were right or not. Peter seemed amused by that. I could hear him snicker with each wrong answer. But I was too preoccupied to care.

Between classes we didn't have much opportunity to talk. There was basically only time to get the books from our lockers and get to the next room. When lunch time finally came, I pulled Reka into an empty hallway.

"Alright. We have to talk about this," I said, keeping my voice hushed in case any stragglers walked by.

"Peter is waiting for me," Reka protested.

"Oh man, you have no idea how much I don't care." The last thing on my mind was Peter's jealousy at the moment. "I need to know more about the council's plans."

"Geez, Cal. I'm not hanging out with them or anything. You know basically what I know."

I could tell she was starting to get defensive. I wondered if my tone was coming off more accusatory than concerning. "Okay. Fair enough," I said, relaxing my eyebrows to make a softer expression. "But how about this: do you know who is on the council?"

"More or less. The council is made up of the twelve major Otherworld creatures around Michigan. Dad—a werewolf, of course—a vampire, imp, fae, banshee, specter, siren, skin walker, wendigo, a jinn, and...um..." She paused and mouthed the names again. "Oh yeah, and two gargoyles."

I buried my face in my hands, blacking out the world to think. There were some powerful creatures on the council. The concern was, the most powerful magical creatures were also the most untrustworthy. Jinn had great power but were notorious for being deceitful and thinking of humans as lower life forms. And even though my mother was a fae, and a good one, I had to admit they were mischievous beings. I certainly wouldn't want to trust a memory altering spell to vampires till I got to know them.

Reka's fingers pulled mine off my face. She looked concerned.

"Hey, don't you think we have enough to worry about on our own?" Reka said. "We got school, home, and you know, being creatures the humans would hunt down with torches and pitchforks if they knew who we really were. Why are you getting so stressed over Jonathan, Tiffany, and Daniel? They're the ones sticking their snotty noses into our business. What happens is their fault."

I nodded. "Maybe, but then again, I'm the one they've been grilling the last few days. Maybe the council wouldn't be worried about them if it wasn't for me. Besides, they aren't bad people, just curious."

"And how do you know they aren't? They have been curious about us and Lana's boarding house for years."

"I just know. It's hard to describe." I didn't feel like going into my whole empathy powers at the moment. "How does the council make decisions?"

"They take a vote, majority rules."

"Hmm…" That gave me some hope. Maybe the council would see reason. Specters in particular tended to be level headed and fair. "Do you know what way your father is planning to vote?"

"Are you kidding me?" Reka rolled her eyes. "I have no idea what he's planning the majority of the time. I really doubt he's biting the bit to tell me either."

"Do you think you could at least try to get a sense of him; try to figure it out?"

She ran fingers through her hair and looked at me for what seemed like minutes. "Fine," she finally said. "I'll give it a try, but no guarantees, okay?"

I smiled. "That's great. Thank you so much!"

"Yeah, yeah, but seriously, don't get your hopes up." Her eyes shifted back down the hallway. "Now, let's head back to the cafeteria and get some food before they close down the kitchen."

"Yeah, wouldn't want that."

Chapter Fifteen

REKA

Man, Calastair threw me a curve. My father sat on the opposite side of the dinner table in our kitchen. I stared at him with so many questions running through my head.

Raz sat on Dad's left, and Adelina, Papo's wife, to his right. My sister, Zrinka, sat between me and Raz and sipped on a glass of iced tea but there wasn't a plate in front of her. I wondered why she was at the table if she had no intention of eating. Papo stood at the stove and sliced steaming cornbread. He was a good cook and often did dinner duty when Zrinka had the night off. So why was she here?

"Did you eat already?" I asked Zrinka as I lifted a platter of fried chicken to offer her.

She waved her hands. "No thanks. I did eat, first shift with the rest of the pack. Peter came in with David and Sorin. He seemed upset. Why didn't you eat with him? You two okay?"

And here we go. That was quick. "We aren't sewn together at the hip, Zrinka. And we don't always eat together. I'm sure he just has this whole thing with the human kids on his mind, like me and the rest of the pack."

"Not me," my sister said. "I'm never updated on pack issues. Right, Dad?"

I looked at my father. He didn't respond to my sister's comment, so I did. "Do you know Johnathan, Daniel, and Tiffany, Zrinka?"

"The three geeks at school?"

That set me back. I didn't think my sister went anywhere near the school.

"Yeah," I said. "Seems they've been hangin' across the street from Lana's, scoping the boarding house out."

"Ah," Zrinka said. "I've been taking a computer class at the high school on Saturday mornings, so I can help do the pack books. They hang out there occasionally. Daniel teaches the class. But they never talk to me."

"No kidding!" *So, my sister does have an outside life.* I made a mental note to tell Peter. My stomach growled. I forked a piece of chicken.

Adelina rubbed her big belly. "The little guy is kicking like playful pup tonight."

"Sure it isn't the little girl?" Papo poked as he wrapped a towel around a basket of cornbread.

They didn't have a sonogram because the pack women home birthed. In case of an emergency, we knew a shifter physician that had access to a facility, one of those rapid in and out surgery centers, and all we had to do was call. She had an excellent staff of mixed Otherworld creatures. A small group; very efficient.

Buddy nosed my calf and scratched for attention. I slipped him a small chunk of chicken under the table and totally ignored my sister's glaring eyes. She didn't like me feeding Buddy table scraps.

"Nope," Adelina said. "but whatever, I think we're gonna have an alpha in the family."

"Hey, yea, aanother female alpha," Raz said.

Zrinka spit a sip of tea through a laugh. "I hope not. One in the family is enough." She smiled at me as she picked Buddy up and placed him in her lap. He tried to paw his way up to her chest to get table access, but my sister gently coaxed him back down.

Papo laid a platter on the table and I shoveled potatoes onto my plate.

Buddy jumped off Zrinka's lap and skittered away.

Zrinka squeezed her eyes into a glare.

"Whatever sex this babe is," Adelina said, "it kicks like a football player."

"How did your meeting with the coven go last night, Dad?" I asked loudly, and bit off half the meat on a chicken leg.

Papo laid a slice of cornbread on my plate, cocked an eyebrow, and tightened his lips in an attempt to make me watch my words. He looked funny and knew it. I gave him a poke and giggled.

"A sudden interest in pack business, Reka?" my father said and seemed put-out. Probably for discussing the geeks with my sister.

Papo winked and mouthed, 'told you so.'

Dad reached for the gravy, covered his mashed potatoes, and passed it to Raz.

With a smirk, my sister set her glass down and answered Dad's question for me. "No. Of course Reka's not interested in pack business, Dad. Like Peter, she's just worried about the kids in school."

Man, I seriously wanted to slap her. I gritted my teeth and considered tossing the chicken leg at her. Instead, I said, "The kids in town are pack business, Zrinka."

Zrinka, eyes on our father, leaned back in the chair and picked up her iced tea. She tongued the straw, nibbled on it, and then took a sip.

"So, Dad, are they going to do the mind wipe?" I boldly asked.

Papo placed the half empty basket of cornbread on the table and took the seat between me and Dad. "I wondered the same thing, Reka. But didn't ask out of respect. I figured your father would want to share that information with everyone at the next meeting."

The last three words resonated in my mind. With all the Cal talk today, I had almost forgotten about the meeting. But that wasn't causing the tension tonight. It was me.

"Sorry, Dad. I kind of egged her on," Zrinka said.

"Oh, please. You don't egg me on. In fact, I asked to keep from talking to you," I taunted Zrinka.

"Exactly!" Zrinka said with a chuckle. "Do I know you, or what?"

I bared my teeth, chicken hanging from my mouth.

"Lovely," my sister said. "No wonder you don't have tons of friends at school; oh, mysterious one with a purple streak in your hair and bad table manners."

My father shot me and Zrinka a parenting scowl. He sliced a hunk of chicken breast off the bone, and, as he set the steak knife down, spoke to Papo. "The meeting actually went well. The coven leaders consented to a mind *reading* instead of a melt...for now. *Everyone* agreed. We should at least find out what they know before we schedule a wipe." Dad caught my eyes with his. "*Unless* what they know is urgent. It takes time and a quiet, safe place to do all three at once, which is preferred."

Raz elbowed me and nodded at an overflowing dish of bacon. Wolves were carnivores and we liked meat, cooked or kicking. There was usually two selections with every meal. The men also loved their mashed potatoes. Tonight, the potatoes were dotted with half-melted chunks of cheddar cheese.

"Hopefully there's *not* going to be a mind wipe," I said, and snagged three bacon strips.

"There will be if it's necessary," Dad said. "And even then, under the supervision of several council members. For right now Castifyn and two other vampires will delve into each of their minds and dig around, see if they're a legitimate threat to us above grounders. If not, we leave them alone. Granted, they may feel a little confused and maybe concerned when three adults approach them during the computer fundraiser this week at the high school. I hear the three of them will be serving refreshments that night. However, Castifyn is quite swift at mind digging in a public place. It will be easy and relatively unnoticeable."

"The coven mind wipers are used to this procedure," Papo assured me, "and rarely have an issue with humans."

The inferior race.

"Watch out, Zrinka," I said. "You never know when a vamp could be checking that hollow place in your head you call a brain."

I snickered at her furrowed brow, and the corners of her turned down mouth. I wanted to tease a bit harder, but something Cal had said pushed me to respond. "The procedure reeks invasion of privacy. It's worse than someone standing outside my bedroom window while I undress. Really, Dad, it's not right. My thoughts are mine. The council has no right—"

"We have every right, Reka," Raz said. "For the same reason police protect and enforce safety among humans. There's nothing to it. It's hypnotism on steroids."

"It doesn't hurt them like human punishment for breaking a law," Adelina added as she patted my hand.

"And the wipe, should they need it, is quick and efficient," Dad said. "Once they remove any incriminating knowledge and the desire to poke around, they will never again question the validity of what we are and what we are capable of."

"Holy wolf's bane! The vampires can really do that to us, too?" I was beginning to see Cal's point.

"Some of us, yes but you need not concern yourself with this," Dad answered.

"No?" My heart accelerated. "Crap like this could change the world." I felt a trickle of sweat on my forehead, and my voice was a little too harsh for dinner table conversation. "What if you decide I'm not towing the line and have my rebellious nature...exorcised, altered?"

No frigging way! I am so out of here if I even think that could happen.

"The Castifyn coven also answers to the council, and the council answers to higher powers Down Under, as we all do," Raz said and picked up his glass of milk. "Much like humans in a court of law. Only, punishment Down Under is much more severe." He lifted the milk glass in a salute and then drained it.

Instead of biting my cornbread, I waved it at my father and frowned. "No one should be allowed to take someone's knowledge or beliefs from them. That's huge. How would any of you feel about being wiped of your lust for the hunt, your need to be free in the woods, our ability to know our second nature?"

"Oh, stop. It's not like they do domestic, artistic, likes or dislikes, or even child-father issues. This isn't about family feuds, a person's personality, or changing a their soul, Reka. It's about us feeling safe to be the creatures we are, and not scaring the shit out of the humans among us. And that won't kill them." Raz lowered his head. A warning. I wasn't just disrespecting my father but our alpha in front of his pack.

Usually, I'd lower my head, too, but held it high, challenging both of them, mainly because my father was quietly eating and listening.

"I don't like the idea someone can change anything about me," I took a bite of the bread, "especially twelve creatures that barely know me. That's not right."

"Do you even listen to the lessons in civics class?" Zrinka asked. "Even the Otherworld has rights."

I bared my teeth and growled this time. Does my sister even hear her own words? I just wanted to scream, 'uh, duh?'

Raz sat stiffly in his chair, fork weighing heavily on a piece of chicken, pressing to the plate. He used his knife to pull the fork out and set the utensils softly beside his plate.

"Our laws are more efficient," Papo said. "And girls, your father would not flippantly allow anyone to mind wipe a pack member, especially his daughters."

"Define flippantly," Zrinka said with a smile.

I snorted.

Dad's shot a glare at me. But when Raz tapped the table with the tip of his fork and then pulled a half smile, Dad relaxed.

"This is not a joking matter, girls," Raz said, eyes going from me to Zrinka and then back to me. "An alpha protects his pack. Period. We're talking about three teenagers making it difficult for us to carry on our daily lives with their constant intrusions and gossip. They're a threat to the whole wolf population. Not just Michigan. And the only reason they're alive is your father is required to protect them in *his* territory."

"So," I tsked. "We're so special—in the human's world, I might add—that we can just wipe their minds to accommodate our needs? Yeah, that's really protecting—"

"Yes!" my father said and slammed his fist on the table. "No one is going to huff and puff and blow their houses down. I won't allow wolves to eat them, or Otherworld beings to threaten them in this city. They crossed the line by knocking on Lana's door *if* they know what she is; I need to be sure they do *before* taking any measure. So, until I confirm their knowledge, if a Down Under creature threatens them, this pack and the rest of the above grounders are willing to die to protect them."

My sister was twirling ice in her glass with a straw. I held back another warning growl because my father's eyes had turned yellow-gold and he was snarling at me, not her.

Papo bent toward me and slipped Buddy another chunk of chicken. His gaze met mine and screamed 'shut up now before it's too late.'

Zrinka, totally unaware of the depth of our father's anger, tsked at Buddy as he licked chicken grease from his maw.

Raz said, "No one is taking advantage of anyone, Reka."

I ground an inch of enamel off my molars.

"Let's all eat," Papo said through a toothy smile. "Before the dinner I worked hard to prepare gets even colder."

Raz scraped up a forkful of gravy smothered potatoes and popped it into his mouth. He pointed the empty fork at my dish. "You gonna finish that cornbread?" he asked.

"So, Dad," I defiantly, but calmly, asked my father, "it's not like your vampire mind-suckers are going to wipe *everything*, right?" I bit a corner off the cornbread while ignoring Raz's steady stare. "I mean, Tiffany, Johnathan, and Daniel won't forget aunts and uncles or how to do algebra or when their birthdays are, or anything like that, right?"

When Dad didn't answer, Raz smiled at me. "Of course not."

Adelina squeezed my hand resting on the table by the fork Raz was still pointing at my cornbread.

Papo laughed. "Finish your bread, Reka. Raz looks like he's waiting for a window of opportunity."

"Why do all of you encourage her?" my father said, glancing around the table, and then turned stern eyes on me. "And why are you asking all these questions? Do you have some sort of kinship with these kids? If you want to be part of pack business, you need to be part of the pack. What if they see one of us shift, snap a photo with their cell phone, and text it to all the kids at the high school? Maybe I should hire guards. Post them around the property. I could assign a couple of them to follow you and Peter around school instead of invading your human friends' private thoughts. Do I restrict you to your bedroom after school, no moonlight runs alone? We wouldn't want one of them to video your jump from the porch and transition midair, would we?"

Dad paused as if waiting for an answer, but I knew he wasn't expecting one. He bit into a bacon slice, chewed forcefully, swallowed hard. "The next time you challenge me, Reka, try to think like a wolf instead of a human. Even your sister is capable of that."

Ugh! "I can't act like an alpha when I'm treated with less respect than my very human sister." I trembled with anger. "You want me to learn? Let Raz or one of the other wolves train me for field work. I'm a good fighter. I'd like a chance to prove that. I want the respect a pack alpha deserves. Or are you worried I may grow to be more powerful than you?"

I couldn't believe I just challenged my father in front of the pack. Everyone in the kitchen—hell, the whole house—became so quiet I heard itty-bitty-critter heartbeats from the basement to the dark corners of attic. Even Zrinka was bug-eyed and slack jawed. I sensed respect and shock. Smelled flight or fight pheromones in the air. And I knew everyone in the room, except my sister, could smell them, too. Even Buddy was wide-eyed silent.

Wolves had some wicked sensory skills. It was painful sometimes. As an alpha, mine were acute.

I stood and pushed the chair out from under me and spurred Buddy into action. He jumped against my leg and I gave his head a scratch.

"I need some fresh air," I said, and turned to my father. His chin was tight but there was a glimmer of pride in his eyes instead of the rage I expected. "Do I need to go upstairs and stick my head out my bedroom window or can I take a run on all fours under the moon?"

"Go," my father said without hesitation, and nodded toward the back porch. "But if you're not home in an hour, I'll personally come looking for you. On all fours."

"Thank you," I said, and turned to go.

"And Reka," Dad said. "I will be happy to begin your training after Peter marks you on your eighteenth birthday. I would have told you sooner, but I didn't think you wanted to stay with the pack. I myself chose to leave the safety of a pack at eighteen, and that's your given right. So, until you make a commitment, I won't waste my time or the energy of my pack to teach you anything."

I wanted to scream but turned, and over my back, said, "If anyone marks anyone, it will be *me* marking the mate of *my* choice." I hit the back door and was running on all four before I could draw a breath into the lungs of my wolf body.

I was confused and frightened when I veered into the woods. Dad didn't react the way I expected.

I was hungry for the warm meat and blood of an animal. I hunkered down and ran. It felt glorious. The cool air, smell of fall, damp earth under my paws. Sniffing the air, my body sensed fear. Something frail and timid exuded it. The air became heavy with a helplessness that only comes from a trapped animal. I followed the scent. As I got closer, I heard a deep throaty growl and the whimper of a human. That changed things. There was only one human on the property, and Zrinka hadn't had time to get this far on human feet. I slowed to a tracker crawl.

A harsh snarl and a scream cut short by a painful yelp spurred me into action. Kicking up dirt, I ran down a deer trail, fur rubbing the brushes on either side. Entering a small plot of open ground by a creek that ran parallel with the paved road located outside our property, I saw her. Blonde, small framed, pink camo sweats, with the jaws of a gray wolf locked around her leg above pink camo tennis shoes. It was Tiffany. Without thinking, I attacked.

The wolf let go, and Tiffany scrambled backward until she hit the trunk of a birch, glaring white in the moonlight. I could smell her fear. My mouth salivated. I snorted away the lust for blood and turned to the wolf. He was a shifter, one I'd never scented, so he wasn't from around here. He was larger than me, but thinner. The hair on his back bristled. I scented fear and anger. A really bad combination.

He softly growled, a threat of ownership, long sharp teeth bared. I could hear Tiffany whimpering behind me, probably as frightened of me as him.

I didn't think past that. Just leapt and was on him in a heartbeat. His teeth snapped at my leg, missed, snapped again, and this time I felt the sharp pain of his bite. We rolled on the ground, he lost purchase on my hind right leg, and I wrapped my maw around the back of his neck, precariously close to his carotid arteries, and bit hard. He violently shook loose and left me spitting wolf hair as he ran toward a road beyond a short, wooded area on the other side of the meadow. Not good.

I stood and licked blood from my front leg. The open sky made it easy for me to follow his path until he disappeared into the woods. The leaves would muck up tracking unless he was bleeding. It would have been easy to hide a vehicle near the road. He'd probably be gone before I got there. A moan from behind reminded me Tiffany was still there.

She tried to get up when I turned but her ankle was clearly broken, and she only made it to one knee. The moon lit a bone poking out of her shin, her pink sweats and tennis shoe covered in blood.

I whimpered and pranced toward her. Tiffany's eyes grew big, her breath rapid. I nudged her hip with my nose. She fell limp and fainted against the tree.

Swell, I couldn't leave her here, and if I took her home, the pack wouldn't let her leave there. She was wolf bit. By morning, Tiffany would begin to feel the pull of the werewolf if the toxin in her blood didn't kill her tonight. I had no choice. Home it was.

I bit into the hood on Tiffany's sweatshirt and dragged her toward a path that led to the house. She was dead weight but would have been harder to drag in human form. In wolf form, my prize was cumbersome but not difficult to move.

Halfway to the house, the wind at my back carried the sounds of another animal behind me. Letting go of Tiffany's hood, I turned my snout to the wind and smelled wolf, a familiar smell this time. It was Peter. I howled and snagged Tiffany's hood. I pulled her to the center of the path, let go, and watched her head bounce on the hard ground. She moaned softly but did not open her eyes as I lapped away dryness on the roof of my mouth and tongue.

Shaking from head to tail, I padded into the woods and limped back out in human form as Peter trotted onto the path. He snarled, fangs exposed, and electric eyes roamed my body and then moved to Tiffany. I could see a second of doubt before his snout tilted up and he whimpered. He'd smelled the other wolf on Tiffany's clothes and the wound on my front leg even though it was under my pants. Peter padded over and nosed the cuff of my jeans, trying to get a better look at the bite. I scratched the back of his ear, patted his rump, then shooed him away and watched him shift.

Bones cracked, skin shrunk, arms filled out as Peter quivered, whimpered, moaned, and panted with the pain of the change. Fur retreated into follicles; claws changed to flat fingernails on the hands of a human. His snout shortened until Peter's face appeared unflawed, black hair sucking up moonlight and firing up cobalt blue streaks. I felt a warmth deep in my stomach. Peter was as handsome a human as he was impressive as a wolf.

I pushed away the desire to run to him, let him wrap his arms around me, and feel the strength I needed right now.

"I had a fight with Dad about the geeks possible mind wipe and came out for a run. When I heard a scream, I didn't know it was Tiffany, but I knew someone was being attacked by an animal. At first I thought bear, but it turned out to be an unknown gray werewolf—didn't know the scent." With a sob choking my words, I turned to Tiffany. "He bit her. Bad. I don't think she can walk."

Peter said, "Let's get her to the house. If the bite doesn't kill her, the leg will be healed by tomorrow night."

"I know," I said. "But will it really matter if she lives? You know the tri-county packs have to vote her in. What if they decide to kill her? It almost makes me want to wish her dead."

Peter shook his head. "Your father won't let that happen. A female? Young enough to breed? I bet your dad lays claim to her very quickly."

"Great," I said, eyes on the ditzy blonde in pink. "I don't think I can live under the same roof with Tiffany."

"Just because your dad lays claim, doesn't mean she can live at the house. She has a human family, relatives, and friends here, and she'll be on the news as a missing person by the weekend."

"Crap." I looked down at the *Barbie Doll* wannabe. "You think she's going to give up her pink jogging suit, designer tennis shoes, gold jewelry, and *Facebook* for a romp in the woods with us during a full moon?" I shook my head and grabbed one of her arms. "Sorry, Peter. I can't see Tiffany in pink camo with a bloody squirrel in her mouth. Can you?"

Chapter Sixteen

C ALASTAIR

I went for a walk after dinner. The chaos of the house was too much for me. The air was crisp, but cool enough to almost feel like water on my cheek. It was refreshing after the stuffy classrooms I'd been in all day. Certainly better than the noise and heat given off from a dozen children in the house.

The day had been stressful. It had been hard to focus on anything the teachers were saying. My mind had been too racked trying to figure out this whole situation with the council. But I had little to show for it. No plan, no action seemed to make things better. Talking to the council of twelve was out. Even if by some mercy my father was okay with me interfering, my voice would carry very little weight. Besides, it was likely they wouldn't even let me speak. On the other end of the spectrum, I couldn't relocate the geeks away from their homes to hide them because I would be interfering more than I already had.

I kicked a stone out of frustration and watched it bounce down the street. As I raised my eyes, they settled on a couple of figures standing near a bike rack. It was hard to make them out in the dim light, but the tall frame of one, and the shorter stouter other looked like Jonathan and Daniel.

For a moment, I thought about turning around before they could spot me. But then I realized for all the worrying and analyzing I'd done about them, we hadn't talked all day. At the very least, it would be a good idea to warn them away from pestering Reka's pack for the near future, or forever if they were smart.

Jonathan looked at me as I approached. "Hey man. How's it going?" he asked with his usual smile. But something was different this time. His voice was tense. Even though he did a good job hiding it, I could feel something was concerning him.

"I'm good. What are you two up to?"

"Oh, not much." His eyes twitched as if he was struggling to keep focus on me.

Daniel checked his cell phone in between glancing around. Something wasn't right.

"Where's Tiffany?" I asked.

Jonathan scratched the back of his head. "Oh, yeah. She's home eating dinner with her family."

He looked nervous and I could sense the lies in his voice. Rather odd they didn't want to tell me. Usually I wouldn't care, but under the circumstances, I wanted to make sure they weren't going to do something stupid.

I narrowed my eyes at Jonathan. "You look concerned. What's up?"

"Nothing."

"Jonathan, where's Tiffany?"

"I told ya—"

"Yeah, and I don't buy it." My tone shifted to sound more serious.

Jonathan looked annoyed at my prodding. "Look, don't worry about it, okay?"

His secrecy sent up immediate red flags. Since I'd arrived the three had been the most open people I'd talked to. Yeah, sure, they were a bit strange, but they always seemed more eager to bring me into their group than keep me at arm's length. And they were a constant presents, albeit transparently pumping me for information about Reka's family, seemed genuinely friendly. So why all the sudden was he so tight lipped?

"Come on, guys," I said as friendly as I could. "I thought I was part of your group. Don't cut me out. What's going on?"

A smile flashed across Johnathan's face. It was the first time since we'd talked that I had acted as part of their group. It seemed to mean a lot to him.

"Alright," he said hesitantly, "she's...ya know, in the woods."

"What woods?" I looked around. The area looked familiar. It suddenly dawned on me that we were near where Reka had told me she lived. Her dirt road jutted off the street we were currently on, almost hidden by the trees. "Those woods?!"

"Yeah," Johnathan said sheepishly.

"You got to be kidding me!" I grabbed my fiery red hair and paced on the sidewalk. I'd spent the whole day trying to figure out a way to keep them out of the council's way, and then they just started poking at them with the biggest sticks they can find!

Johnathan raised his palms. "Whoa, relax, bro. What you so worked up about?"

"I'm worked up because you guys must be the stupidest people I've ever met! I mean, what the hell were you thinking?" I lashed out but regretted it when I saw Johnathan's expression droop like a scolded child.

Daniel stepped up. "What's your problem?! We go in there all the time. It's not a big deal. I'm pretty sure a good chunk of it is state land."

"If it's not a big deal, why did you look so concerned when I walked up?"

Daniel's scowl softened. "It's nothing. Just...Tiffany said she'd meet us here a half hour ago." He poked at his phone's screen. "For some reason, she's not picking up my calls."

I sighed. In my mind, I could see the pack of werewolves circling her, nipping at her ankles. Teeth bared and drool sliding off the snarled lips. I should have never even talked to these three about Reka and her family.

"Okay, look," I said, making eye contact with Johnathan. "I'll go find Tiffany. You guys head home. I'll let ya know when I find her."

Johnathan opened his mouth to protest, but I shut him down quickly. "If she was caught trespassing on their property, trust me when I say it's better if you two are nowhere near the place."

Daniel crossed his arms. "And what if *you* get caught?"

"I've been hanging with Reka lately. I'll just tell them I'm there to see her. They'll be fine with it." That was a bold-faced lie, but thanks to my mother's fae blood, I was good at it.

The two exchanged glances. Daniel shrugged, but didn't have any objections.

"Alright. We'll leave it to you," Johnathan said. "Just tell Tiffany to text us when she can, and we'll figure it out from there. Sound good?"

I nodded, and the two headed down the street. When they finally disappeared from view, I slipped into The Gray. Now invisible to human eyes, I veered quickly into the woods.

I searched as hastily as I could. My tracking abilities where subpar at the best and being in the world of black and white wasn't helping. But I dared not leave The Gray just in case any of Reka's pack were roaming the woods for a late-night hunt.

After a half hour, I became impatient. The woods were too large for me to search by myself. *Wait*, I thought. *I don't have to look through the entire area, I just have to make sure she's not caught by the family.*

Of course, to do that I would have to enter their house. It was something I would have liked to avoid, especially after Reka showed some ability to detect me while I was in The Gray. If her family had similar senses, there was a risk of being discovered, but I had to be sure.

I hurried down the dirt road. It thinned till it was no thicker than a driveway. At the end of the road, an old looking log cabin stood. It had a wooden deck, crudely made, and parts of the siding was torn. Tools and random junk littered the front yard, most of it rusty and worn. The whole spectacle was unwelcoming, but then again, I felt that might be the point.

I stepped in, moving through the walls like they were smoke. No one was in the living room. Old, comfortable furniture filled the space. Their style wasn't that much different than Lana's, except for the hunters' atmosphere and more pictures on the wall.

I floated up the stairs, keeping an open ear to any movement. I heard soft voices from down the hall. Focusing on them, I realized one was Reka. Her voice was hushed and dampened by the door. There was also a male voice inside. It took me a moment to realize it was Peter. *It's getting late. What's Peter doing in Reka's room? Ohh.* I became uncomfortable. Maybe I shouldn't go in there. To make sure I wasn't interrupting anything inappropriate, I leaned into the door just enough for my ear to pass through to the other side.

"Keep pressure on it," I heard Peter say. "It's got to clot up soon."

"It should have stopped by now." Reka's voice sounded distressed. "How tight did you clamp the wound?"

I peeked the rest of my head through the door. Reka stood by her bed, blood smeared over her white shirt. Peter was there beside her, and on the bed laid a unconscious Tiffany. Blood seeping through a towel wrapped around her leg.

"Tight enough. You should call your dad," Peter said, his voice was calm and controlled.

"No. I don't want to bring him into this unless we have to. Things are bad enough."

Peter didn't look convinced. "He's been through this kind of thing more than anyone. Anytime anyone gets wolf bitten he always handles—"

Wait, WHAT?! I pulled back the curtain of realities and poked my head out of The Gray. "Tiffany got bit by a werewolf?!"

Both of them almost jumped out of their shoes. Reka reached up and grabbed my ear. With a strong yank, she pulled me the rest of the way out of The Gray and threw me on to the floor. "Stop doing that!!"

"Sorry." I stood up, rubbing my ear.

"What the hell? You can turn invisible?!" Peter asked.

"Well, that's an extreme simplification of it."

Peter's expression darkened. "And is this what you do with it; perv around girls' bedrooms?"

I couldn't help but snarl at Peter. "No, you jackass." I pointed at Tiffany. "I came looking for her! What happened?"

Reka looked at Tiffany. I could see concern in her eyes. "I found her when I was out for a run. Some werewolf I didn't recognize had her leg in its jaw. She's hurt bad, Cal."

I looked at her leg; her pink pants were torn. Dry and wet blood-stained half of them. It was clear she'd lost a lot of blood. "You sure it was a werewolf?"

"Trust me. I know a werewolf when I see one. I've had a lot of experience."

This could change everything. I knew the curse was transferred through bites. It was already coursing through her veins, infecting her heart. She was already a werewolf. She just didn't know it yet.

"What do you think your dad's going to do?" I asked Reka.

Her eyes dropped. "I...I'm not sure how he'll handle it. But I know he'll find a way to care for her, make her part of our clan. He's always concerned about the lack of fertile females in our pack. But she has her own family; she can't just pack up and leave them."

Peter's muscular hands rested reassuringly on Reka's shoulder. "There's another problem," he said, making eye contact with me. "The other wolf knows it bit her. He may have done it on purpose to try expanding their own pack. If that's the case, they could come looking for her. But to bite her here, on our territory, well, there could be bigger problems, especially if the other wolf tries to claim her. He'd be crazy to do so, but not unlikely. If she doesn't take the turn, then they're still going to want answers. Either way, this could come down to diplomacy." Peter hesitated. "That's not one of our pack leader's specialties."

Reka huffed. "Yeah; brute force is more his style."

This whole situation was spinning out of control.

I knelt down by the bed and rested a hand on Tiffany's wound. Her pulse was rapid and sweat pooled in her blonde hair. I could sense the curse flowing through her, and her body trying to fight it off. It would end one of two ways. Either the body would give in to the curse, or it would burn itself out trying to fight it.

But maybe there was another option.

"I might be able to help her fight off the werewolf curse," I blurted out.

Reka frowned. "That's impossible, Cal."

"No. It's just difficult. But I think I can do it. That is…if my father is willing to help a bit."

Peter leaned over me. "Your father? I don't understand. What are you talking about?"

"I don't have time to explain," I said agitatedly. "If I'm going to do this, the sooner the better. You're going to have to trust me."

"I don't!" Peter blurted.

Reka stared at me a moment. I could see her uncertainty. But she gently placed her hand on Peter's triceps. "Look, it's not going to hurt to try," she said calmly. "If he can't do it, then we're no worse off than we are right now. "

Peter looked unconvinced but nodded. "We're still going to have to deal with the other wolf, and Tiffany's bite."

I couldn't help but feel his resistance had more to do with me than the plan.

Downstairs, I heard a door open and shut.

"Damnit," Reka said with a soft tone. "Someone's home."

I cinched the towel around Tiffany's wound tighter. "I can't do this here anyway. We need to get her back to my place."

"And how do you want to do that?" Peter scoffed. "Even if we could carry her out of the house without anyone seeing, we still have to get her through town."

Reka's eyes lit up. "The Gray! Can you take her into...whatever it is?"

I thought for a moment. It was extremely against the rules to bring a mortal into the guardian angel's realm. Then again, she was unconscious, so she wouldn't be able to see anything. Why not. If I was going to get kicked out of heaven, might as well do it with style.

"I should be able to. It'll take a second, though."

"Okay." Reka put her hands on her hips. "Peter, go downstairs and distract whoever that is. They'll be picking up Tiffany's scent soon, keep them busy. Just tell them you came up for a second to visit. It's late but try to convince them."

Peter still didn't look happy. "Fine, we'll do it your way," he conceded. "But for the record, I think our best bet is to come clean to your dad."

Peter made his way out of the door. For as muscular as he was, he was very light of foot. Peter managed to open the door and close it without making a noise.

"I'm going to need your help getting her through the curtain," I said, already raising my hand to cut through into The Gray. I pulled reality back and held it open with my foot. Reka propped Tiffany up on her shoulder and between the two of us, we managed to set her in The Gray.

"The blood!" Reka started tearing at her sheets. "They'll be able to smell it. Can we throw these in there, too?"

"Yeah, I guess."

Reka handed the bloody sheets to me, and I set them down next to Tiffany. The red stains changed to dark gray as they passed the threshold.

"Ah great. My shirt's covered in blood too." Reka groaned. "Turn around, Cal. I got to put on a clean one."

I did so. There was a rustling behind me and a second later, I saw her shirt fly over my head, landing on Tiffany's arm. I heard Reka dig through one of her dresser drawers.

"Dakota, if you have a second, I would really like to talk about some pack business," Peter's muffled voice resonated from the other side of the door. It sounded desperate to get someone's attention. I saw the doorknob turn out of the corner of my eye, and the door cracked open. Without enough time to jump into The Gray, I retracted my hands and let the entrance seal.

An older man entered. "Reka, what's going on? I could smell..." His gruff voice tailed off when he spotted me. His eyes shifted from me, to Reka who frantically pulled her new shirt down over her stomach. The man's eyes lit on fire and turned back to me. It didn't take someone with empathic abilities to figure out what he was assuming.

An uncomfortable silence fell on the room.

"Hey. I bet you're Reka's Dad," I said, upbeat, trying to hide how nervous I was. "Now I know what you're thinking, but it's not like that, I swear."

Before I could blink, the man leapt across the room, grabbed me, and pinned me to the wall. His bared teeth inches from my face.

"I wasn't born yesterday," Reka's father growled. "Don't try that bullshit on me. You come into my house without my permission, into my daughter's bedroom!"

I offered as little resistance as I could, not wanting to escalate the situation. "No...well, yes...I guess I did. But we weren't doing anything, I promise."

"Let him go, Dad!" Reka said from across the room.

His right hand let go of my arm and grasped my throat. "I should snap your neck, boy." He hissed as his hand tightened.

It was hard to breathe. "Alright. I didn't want to do this," I wheezed. I balled a fist with my right and sent it into his side. However, it felt like it made contact with a stone wall.

If the punch had caused any pain, he didn't show it. The only effect was an increase of rage in the man's eyes.

So, I don't have my angelic strength. Good to know.

He twisted around and threw me out the open door and into the hallway wall. My shoulder punched a hole in the drywall. Pain radiated down my arm like I'd never felt before.

I quickly got up and tore down the hallway past a startled Peter. I could hear Reka's dad was right behind me. I dodged through the furniture in the living room and burst out the front door. He chased me to the bottom of the steps and stopped.

"I don't care who you are!" he shouted after me. "And I don't care if you're under Lana's care or not. If you ever come back here, I'll kill you, understand?!"

I did, and I believed him.

I ran till I was hidden by the night. After I was sure he could no longer see me, I ducked into The Gray and hurried back to their house. Reka's dad's yelling could be heard from the outside. It gave me pause. Even though I was invisible in The Gray and safe from harm, his voice was still intimidating.

I hurried up the stairs and back into Reka's room. Tiffany laid there, visible to only me, with the bloody sheets and shirt. Reka sat on her bed while her dad launched into a tirade, mostly about me. Part of me wanted to help, but there wasn't much I could do. She would have to battle this alone.

I grabbed Tiffany and tucked her to my chest. My injured shoulder protested, but I was able to fight through the pain. I gathered the linen as well and, silently wishing Reka luck, hurried back to Lana's.

THE JOURNEY WAS TIRING, and everything ached by the time we got there. Tiffany's breaths had grown erratic. Every intake of air caused a wheezing sound to escape her lungs. I could feel heat radiating off her forehead onto my chest. She was burning up. It didn't seem like she was going to stop fighting the curse, and she couldn't take much more of this.

I stayed in The Gray all the way to my room, trying not to attract any attention from Lana or anyone else in the house. After checking to make sure no one was in my doorway, I busted back into the color of the human's reality and set Tiffany gently on my bed. I closed my door and grabbed my father's note off my desk.

"I know you've been watching, and I'm sure there's a lot you want to lecture me about, but there isn't time now. You got to restore my powers to heal."

The note remained blank for a moment, then the silver letters appeared

You never finished your training. This may be beyond you.

"Thanks, I'm aware," I said through gritted teeth. "But I've got to try. Or you could come down and do it yourself."

The letters disappeared, but none replaced them. I began to worry my father was going to deny my request when the room began to spin. I let go of the note and grabbed my desk to support myself. Once it passed, I looked again at my father's letter on the floor.

Be smart, be careful, be safe.

I hurried to Tiffany's side. It had been a while since I'd worked with my healing abilities, and my father was right, I was hardly an expert at it. So, I decided I would start with the bite wound. I carefully unwrapped the towel around her leg. Peeling it off, I saw the lacerations for the first time. The skin around each puncture was black and red. Blood bubbled up the wounds now that they were unhindered by the makeshift bandage.

I placed my hand over the bite. The area was as hot as Tiffany's forehead. I closed my eyes and focused. A cool energy began to grow in my stomach. It was the energy angels used to heal. It was fueled by the same power that produces the spark of life, just not as powerful.

I focused and stoked the energy. It grew till it was large enough to heal Tiffany's wound. I began moving it up through my chest and toward the hand I laid on her leg, directing it through my body as a human would tighten a muscle. Once it reached my hand, it shot off my body like a ray of light.

Tiffany's skin cooled under its power. After the light faded, I withdrew my hand to see the bite had healed. The only hint it ever existed was a small mole in the shape of a wolf paw, smeared blood, and torn pant legs.

I smiled to myself. *Guess I'm better at this than I thought.* However, the hard part still laid ahead.

Tiffany continued to struggle to breathe. The curse still affected her. In order to save her, I would have to draw it out like poison. During my training, we practiced with minor curses, never anything as powerful as a werewolf. I could only hope that because it hadn't fully taken over, I would be able to draw it out.

I placed my hand over Tiffany's chest. I closed my eyes and let my senses flow into her. There I could see the curse circling her heart. It was like tendrils of smoke prodding, squeezing, and trying to get in. I once again called the healing energy back to my hand. This time I brought it to my fingertips and extended it into her chest. I held the energy in place and waited for a time to strike. As soon as a tendril of the curse flowed close to my fingertips, I closed down trying to grab it, but it slipped out of my grasp like a fish through a fisherman's hands.

I regathered my focus and tried again. The same result. Now the curse seemed to be anticipating my actions. It was just too quick for me to grasp. But a thought occurred to me. Since it originated in her leg, it would have moved up to her chest from there. I moved my fingers down from her heart toward her navel. Some of the dark energy was still there, but it was more dormant than the tendrils around the heart.

Before the curse could sense what I was doing, I lunged once again and grabbed hold of the smoke and used the healing energy to pull it out of her body and into my hand. I opened my eyes to see the black cloud pooling in my palm. Its tendrils still snagged in Tiffany's body.

The curse fought back, latching harder onto her heart. Tiffany started convulsing. Her arms flailed about, smacking into the wall and knocking things off my nightstand. Her head arched backward, and chest pushed out as if the smoke yanked her upward.

I pulled again and more of the curse billowed out of her chest. Another pull, the same result. I was successfully drawing it out, but the tendrils were still hooked deep. I began to worry I wouldn't be able to pull the whole thing before it killed Tiffany. But I also knew that with her weakened state, if I let go, the curse would take hold of her heart easily. My mind raced as I began to panic.

The light I had been producing from my palm flickered as I lost concentration. The curse grew stronger. The smoky tendrils above her chest swirled and formed a wolf's head. The creature lunged forward and snapped its wispy teeth at me.

Startled, I jerked back, giving the curse an opportunity to dig back into Tiffany. Its head burrowing back into her chest.

My mind raced, franticly looking for answers. I recalled one of my father's lessons. *Remember son*, he said, kneeling next to my young self. *Curses are a powerful force. But all they can do is alter life. The powers we wield can sustain life, even when it seems hopeless.* He rested his hand on my chest. *Thus, every curse or dark entity will always fear the light you can conjure in here. And when they become afraid, they act more aggressive. But it is a façade. You will be able to overcome them, as long as you stay calm and trust your abilities.*

The wolf buried itself deeper into Tiffany's chest. I took a deep breath and concentrated. Alright, I needed to stay calm, trust my abilities. I could do that. Centering myself, I focused once again on the energy in my palm. The flickering stopped, and it shined brighter. If the curse had too strong of a grip on her heart, then it was time to loosen it.

I intensified the light till it shot through the smoke in my hand. The wolf's head reeled up in pain and it lost its grip. I took the opportunity and pulled hard, yanking the rest of the curse out of Tiffany.

The wolf turned its full attention on me. Still within my grasp, its tendrils formed into paws with sharp claws. They swiped at me, its teeth gnashed inches from my face. Even though it was smoke, my mind imagined the creature's hot breath.

I heard my door open and Lana scream, "Mary and Joseph! What are you doing in here?!"

"I'm a little busy, Lana. Be with you in a second," I said, dodging another snap of its jaws. I focused all the energy I had left into my hand. It grew brighter and brighter, till it nearly fully engulfed the darkness. With one last screech, the curse exploded into sparks of light. All of its tendrils burning away like embers in the wind.

Exhausted, I collapsed onto my knees. I looked at Tiffany. Her hair and forehead were coated in sweat, but her breathing had returned to normal. She looked like she was going to make it.

I looked up at Lana, whose expression laid somewhere between shock and anger. "I suppose you have some questions?" I said, wiping beads of sweat from my brow.

Chapter Seventeen

REKA

Peter stepped into my bedroom a few minutes after my father ran out following Cal. "Nice work. Why was your blouse off?"

"Why didn't you come in and give me a little help?" I shot back. "I saw you out in the hall."

"Yeah. Like that would've calmed your father down. You had a, a, whatever in your bedroom, and you were getting dressed! What the hell, Reka?

"Cal wasn't watching, or didn't you notice? I took off my bloody blouse and tossed it into The Gray with Tiffany. I was pulling on another when you two opened the door. I told you to take care of whoever was down there."

"No one 'takes care' of your father."

"You should've defended me, if not downstairs, at least up here."

Before Peter could reply, Dad burst into the room again. He glanced at Peter and glared at me. "Explain yourself. No one is allowed on the property, never mind into our home, without an invitation from—"

"I invited him," Peter blurted. "I was in the room the whole time until I came down to meet you."

We both turned to Peter.

"I dragged him up here because he came looking for Tiffany. Daniel and Johnathan told Cal she was headed here to find Reka."

"Why?" my father asked. "You didn't tell her anything about the mind wipe, vampires, or the council, did you?"

My father was trembling mad.

"Of course not!" I shouted.

"It wasn't like that," Peter said. "We were going to search for Tiffany to tell her Cal didn't have a crush on Reka and that Reka and I were..." He swallowed hard, and his eyes grazed mine. "...hooked. Tiffany likes Cal."

"More than likes," I added.

My father stared at me, his brow furrowed, eyelids squinty.

"Cal is my friend," I said. "Both of you need to get over that because he's going to remain my friend. You owe him an apology, Dad. You owe me one, too. You don't trust me. That's unacceptable." Heck, that was a stupid remark after the lies I'd just spewed and encouraged Peter to put out. I wondered if karma entertained apologies.

My father's jaw tightened. He gritted his teeth, and his eyes flashed gold, again, for the umpteenth time today. Not good. I bit my lips together and held them shut.

Dad ran a hand over his head, finger-combing long black waves away from his face. "You still haven't explained why you were pulling your blouse down in front of him when I walked in."

"If you both weren't being jerks, you might have asked before you scared the shit out of him." *Oh my god, will I ever just shut my mouth?*

"Watch your language, Reka," Dad said with a growl. "I was a boy once. Being invited into a girl's bedroom, no matter the circumstance, was an invitation to—"

"Ugh!" I spat, all thoughts of lies and karma retribution out the window. "First, you burst into my room, and then accuse me of, of... And then accuse Cal of thinking like an ass like you. Your way of thinking about women is deplorable. How could you think like that?"

I took a deep breath and hissed it out. "I'm not sexually active, Dad. And don't either of you smile. It's not because you expect that, but because I'm not ready. And, I'm not going anywhere or doing anything stupid until I'm eighteen and can legally make my own decisions...and in return be accountable for them. Even though I still haven't made up my mind about Peter's mark, I would never be unfaithful to him or your command, until I am considered, by law, an adult. Even then..."

Peter stood beside my father, and his expression was priceless.

"I do love and respect you, Peter. I'm just not sure it's... Look, I'm not ready to think about a mate. I'm still trying to figure out who I am, what makes me smile, and if I want this kind of life."

"Reka!" my father shouted, hands balled at his hips. "Stop deflecting! There is no other life. You're not human. Why were you pulling down your blouse?"

I huffed, lowered my head, and stared at the floor. "Because Cal thought he saw me cutting myself at school and I was showing him I did no such thing."

I felt like the gooey scum hanging onto the inside of the metal elbow under my sink drain. I hated lying.

"Smart," Dad said. "It would be healed by now. But I'm sure Calastair didn't know that."

"Did you cut yourself?" both Peter and Dad asked.

I frowned. I didn't feel so scummy now. I'd just told Peter what *really* happened. Why was he asking again?

"No!" I answered. "As a matter of fact, I haven't cut myself since I met Cal." I turned to my father. "Cal is just a friend and showing him my stomach is like showing you."

I pulled up my shirt to the middle of my bra. Wolves were not shameful of their body, especially in the company of pack or another werewolf. Peter rolled his eyes.

Dad's shoulders relaxed, but I wasn't expecting an apology—didn't want one. I'd lied to him. He confirmed my expectation when he abruptly turned and headed for the door. "How werewolves feel about their bodies is not acceptable to most in the human world, Reka. That boy might have gotten the wrong idea."

Dad stepped through the threshold and looked back over his shoulder. "I don't ever want to see a male of any species in your bedroom unless he is your...proposed mate. Do I make myself clear?"

"So freaking obnoxiously," I said. At least he hadn't ruled out the creature or sex of said mate.

"Good. And Peter," my father turned in his direction, "pick up the crap laid all over the front lawn and tell Sorin and David to get some mowing in before all the leaves fall off the trees. If we are going to have outside visitors..."

"I'm sure Calastair thinks we live like a bunch of animals," Dad said and closed the door behind his words.

"Damn," Peter said. "You think he meant inviting Cal over is acceptable now that he knows?"

"I doubt Cal will want to come over after tonight." I mulled over my part in his almost getting his butt kicked.

Peter smiled and I almost hated him for it. Almost. I had to smile.

"I hope Tiffany is alright," I whispered.

My father had exceptional hearing, but in his mood, I doubted he was using that skill right now. No need to be careless, though.

"I'm just as worried about your dad finding out about the wolf on our property as I am about Tiffany being alright," Peter said so softly I barely heard it. "I mean, think about it, Reka. You just lied to your father. Multiple freaking times. And we're both betraying the pack by not telling them about the rogue wolf biting a human. Is that who we are now?"

"Yeah, I did lie. And no, I hope I'm not digressing to that kind of person. I'll admit that's pretty big." I had an almost uncontrollable urge to slice the skin over my knee and watch it bleed. "I'm hoping we'll have an opportunity to make up for this after we find out if Tiffany actually lived through the wolf bite. Whether she's a wolf, or dead, we'd have something to go to Dad with."

"So, you think that's gonna help? Nothing is going to make up for the fact we lied and covered up a threat to our pack. Maybe if we go down there right now and tell him the truth—"

"We cannot do that without giving up Cal," I said. "Think about it. We don't even know what Cal is. That he thinks he can prevent a werewolf bite from infecting a human is even bigger than the wolf biting a human on our property. You do realize what that would mean? Heck, that in itself is a reasonable explanation for holding back a day, one Dad is sure to understand."

"Yeah, Cal would be a big consideration for the council and everything that is Down Under if he was capable of healing us," Peter said. "Would you rather be human? Because I sure wouldn't."

I had not been thinking along those lines. Not only would Cal be a threat to our breed but the existence of everything that is Down Under. What else was he capable of?

"There's a balance the gods try to maintain, Reka. Your new friend is capable of destroying that balance. Powers more significant than us would not be happy with some vigilante creature, mercy on his mind, who doesn't get the reasons we do things the way we do Down Under."

"Wow. I'd say we have several major issues here," I barely said aloud.

"How are you feeling about being old enough to handle things now, Reka?" Peter said, his voice a level higher than before. "Are you as ready to accept who you are, what an alpha's obligations are in their pack?"

Now Peter was downright loud, like he wanted my father to hear him. Crap. That was a low blow. It's a good thing the bed was right under my butt when I plopped down, mouth open, eyes wide, more blown away by what Peter just said than the volume. I shook my head. "Oh my God, who, and what, is Cal?"

"Yeah, that's right, let that sink in," Peter whispered, "And we're not even telling your dad so he can do something about it. Smart. Really smart, Reka."

"Okay, so we need to talk to Cal."

"Cal? Cal? Is that all you can think about is Cal? Where are your priorities?"

I took a deep breath. "Look, we can handle this, Peter. First thing tomorrow morning we head over and meet Cal. We find out what's going down with Tiffany. Then we make some decisions. I just don't think it's smart to do anything until we're sure we have to.

"If the three of us can handle this, we might be able to thwart a territory war. We need to make Cal understand that maybe having the vampire coven mind wipe the Geek Squad isn't such a bad idea because I'm thinking that could very well be the motive for the rogue wolf attack on Tiffany. And lastly, we sure as heck need to make Cal understand that although we get him wanting to save Tiffany, removing the wolf after a wolf bite is epic, to both the human population and Down Under."

"Yes," Peter said. "And outline how wolves and other creatures help balance and protect the human race. How we keep others like him, a being who can destroy everything for us if it's not using its powers correctly, from doing just that. That's a big task for two seventeen-year-olds, don't you think?"

"What? You're not up for it?" I asked. "This is big. Something I can finally sink my canines into. You do realize as much as it seems bad at the moment, there is a good to it. What a powerful tool to help human kind, and Down Under control the horrors of both species. If he has saved Tiffany from being like us against her will, that is humongous! I want to be a part of that."

"Ugh!" Peter threw his hands up as he walked across the room and sat on the bed beside me. "All I'm saying is, at the moment, your father is our alpha. Doing anything like...well, anything without his knowledge is going against our leader and the safety of our pack."

"Whoa. Step off your platform, wolf. Think about it." I stood facing Peter. "Our alpha is not god. Just our leader. And I agree. If Tiffany doesn't make it," I swallowed hard, fear electrifying the hair on the back of my neck, "then we made a big mistake by waiting.

But if she does live without the wolf inside her, and we can fix this kind of thing with others brutally infected against their will, we need to take that chance."

"You're thinking like a five-year-old," Peter said and stood.

"No. I'm acting like an alpha. An alpha capable of leading a pack before jumping all over it. And I need to prove that to my father."

Peter grabbed both of my shoulders and pulled me to his chest. His breath was hot on my neck as he held me close. I couldn't move, and I didn't want to.

"I love you, Reka" he whispered, breath tickling my ear. "I've always loved you. So, I'm going to go with this because if I want to be your mate, I need to trust you."

The waves of emotions that ran through me at that moment were unexplainable. Respect, and the complete understanding that Peter was a part of me. Whether it be a true friend or the lover I would take on when I was ready, I didn't know. But one thing was obvious. I loved this guy, and I didn't want to live without him.

I took in a deep breath and squeezed him tight. "I love you, too. I'm just not ready to be marked, Peter. Can you give me some time?"

"As much as you need," Peter said, and kissed me softly.

My body leaned into his, and before I could strengthen the kiss, he broke away and held me at arm's length.

With a smile, he said, "I don't think we should wait for morning to talk to Cal. We need to go over there now. Hopefully, we can settle this before morning."

I barely heard his words. I could still feel the heat of his kiss. My hands fell to my sides as I stared into his eyes. But I couldn't let an attraction rule my need to make a point that women could be both a mother and a leader.

"I'm serious," Peter said, mistaking my silence for disagreement.

I cleared my throat and asked, "Do you really think that's a good idea? I mean, Lana is there. What if we wake her? What if we have to tell her why we're there?"

Peter tucked his hands into the pockets of his jeans. "Do you have any other ideas? I know you trust Cal, even if I don't understand why. I have to respect that. But are you sure he won't do something that could further hurt him and us before tomorrow morning? What if he needs help with the...um, body, or—"

"I don't know. Maybe, but he said he would handle it. But my wolf sense tells me he can. And I have to go with it."

"So, you trust him?"

"Um...yes. Look, I can't explain why," I said, my mind searching for doubt. "It's a blind faith kind of trust that I know can be dangerous. But for some reason I don't think so, in this case. I trust him totally. It's like I've known him all my life, or at least I've been searching for him."

Peter stiffened, and I immediately put my hands up. "Hold on, before you go getting all fangs and growls on me. It's not like that. It's something I can't explain. But it's not physical. It's...I don't know what it is. But it's not a girl-guy thing at all."

"Alright, so you have this trusting, soulmate, BFF forever thing going on with somebody you just met, and I'm going to try to understand what that's like. The only soulmate I have is you, and the unconditional thing took years to develop.

"I don't want to stop you from having friends, Reka. But I'm a male wolf, and let's not forget, I'm and alpha too. That automatically makes me, well, in constant battle with myself. So, try to understand it's difficult not to jump into the controlling, protecting mode with all four paws."

"Can you at least try to accept Cal?" I asked. "If it makes you feel any better, I'd probably feel the same way if you had a friend outside the pack. Maybe I'd even uncontrollably and unreasonably want to bite her...um him. Whatever."

Peter smiled. "I'll remember that."

I punched him in the chest playfully and headed for the bedroom door.

"Whoa, hold on." Peter grabbed me by the shoulder. "If we're going to Cal's, I think out the bedroom window, over the roof, and down the oak tree would be the way to go. You?"

"Agreed," I said and climbed out the window, tiptoed across the roof, and leapt. I was on all fours when I hit the ground. Heck, yeah, this alpha could move fast *and* stealthy in her wolf fur.

THE CRESCENT MOON WAS high in the sky as we ran through the woods on four paws. It was windy and brisk, but in the fur that was very pleasant. I don't know what Peter was feeling, but because of the adrenaline rush I had over the whole evening, I was hungry. Trying to curb the strong desire to hunt, I kept Peter's pace until we trotted up to the edge of the woods near town. We stood close, tails up, ears back, noses in the air. I nosed his ear and then give him a lick. He snorted and leaned his body into mine.

Deciding to approach Lana's in wolf form could be a bad move if anyone saw us. Wild animals cruising so close to the houses with humans and pets about was a threat, especially in numbers. Living in a basically rural setting, most people had gun safes. Still, it was better than someone seeing us out and about this late on a school night. We'd phase back when we got to Lana's backyard.

Cal had a corner room over the roof on the back porch. There was a black walnut tree that might give us access to the roof. From there, we'd tap softly on his bedroom window if it wasn't open.

When we got to Lana's, every light in the house was out. It looked totally black inside, not even a soft ray from a nightlight. We padded up the stairs, and I sat on my haunches and watched Peter make a quick walk around the back-porch, nose to the wood planking below his paws. When he made it back around my side of the porch, his ears up, tail wagging, tongue hanging out of his mouth, I figured all was good. I leaped on and over a small stack of fireplace wood, and before I hit the porch on the way back down, I stood on two legs. Peter took off to some bushes in the corner of the backyard.

Walking the porch, I found a window cracked a couple of inches. There was no doubt we could get up the tree and on to the tin roof, but noise wise, it would be better going in the window instead of jumping from the tree to the roof on two feet.

About five minutes later, which seemed like five hours, Peter jogged toward the house. I pointed at the cracked window, and without a word, we pushed it up high enough to climb through. We were in a small mudroom with a washer and dryer off the kitchen.

We walked past a long, wooden coat rack with a bunch of shoes and boots lining the wall beneath it. I stepped through an arch into a hall and Peter followed. On the right was the porch door. I unlocked it. An old, French, glass door on the left gave entrance to the kitchen. It was locked with a skeleton key from the other side.

"Swell," I whispered.

"Hang on," Peter said and walked back into the mudroom. I watched him searching the shelves over a sink on the back wall, and then some drawers in the cabinet beside the sink. He moved from there to a ledge on the wall near the window and finally came back my way with an ice pick.

"Let's try this," he said.

A skeleton keyhole was a circle, open at the bottom in the shape of a fat squatty triangle to let the paddle on the key move the lock to enter. Ancient and easy to pop. There was no bolt lock installed. I hoped Lana thought a chain lock wasn't necessary on the other side of the door.

With no street lights in front of Lana's house, it was pitch black in the kitchen as Peter worked on the lock. But even in human form, werewolves had night vision. In no time, I heard the lock tumble. It's a good thing crime wasn't as high back when these locks were made.

Peter quietly turned the crystal doorknob, and we stepped into the kitchen. I made a mental note to suggest Lana invest in a bolt lock.

"What now?" I softly whispered before a blinding light assaulted.

A silhouetted figure, backlit by an open refrigerator, asked, "What are you two doing here?"

Chapter Eighteen

CALASTAIR

I sat on the floor, trying to catch my breath. Fighting with the werewolf curse took more out of me than I thought.

Lana looked down at me. Her expression changed from surprise to anger. She reached down, grabbed the same ear Reka used to pull me out of The Gray, and yanked me up on my feet. "Calastair, what did you do?!"

"Ahhh...can you at least tug on the other ear? That one's already been through a lot tonight."

"No!" Lana gave it a warning twist. "Now, explain yourself!"

"Alright, alright." I broke free from her grasp and took a few steps back, just in case she didn't like my answer. "I went over to Reka's. When I got there, she and Peter told me Tiffany had been bitten by some random werewolf on their property. So I brought her here to draw the curse out of her."

Lana placed her hands on her hips. "Why did you bring her here? Couldn't you have done it there?"

"I didn't want to risk one of the other pack members walking in and seeing anything. Plus, Reka's dad objected to me being there." I instinctively rubbed the shoulder that was thrown into the wall. It still ached.

Lana shot daggers from her eyes. "So, you decided to bring her here, to my house with children, and do a risky procedure without telling me?"

It honestly didn't occur to me to tell Lana about my plans. "Well, to be fair, you already have some scary ass children here. And I didn't think you'd have a problem with it."

Lana took a step forward. I cupped my ear with my hand. "Of course I have a problem with it, Cal! This house is a sanctuary. I don't get involved in others' affairs, and they stay out of mine! What if the pack that bit her tracks her here?"

I scoffed at the idea. "I brought her through The Gray. Even a werewolf wouldn't be able to track her in there. They'll follow the trail to Reka's house. Which is bad, but there's not much I can do about that. Unless maybe—"

"You're missing the point, Cal!" Lana stomped her foot against the shag carpet. "This is neutral ground. We don't get involved with pack politics. And exorcising the werewolf curse from someone definitely counts."

I looked at Tiffany. She looked peaceful laying there; almost seemed hard to believe just a few minutes ago she was fighting for her life. "Sorry, Lana. I suppose I should have told you what I was doing. I didn't mean to get you involved. It just...didn't seem right to leave her there."

Lana sighed and shook her head. "Well, I guess what's done is done. Just try to think things through in the future." She tapped a flaking bright red finger nail against my head and knelt down next to Tiffany. "How's she doing?"

"I think she'll be okay. But it was a rough exorcism; probably will be sleeping for a while."

Lana felt her forehead and took her pulse. "Did your father know you were going to do this?"

"He gave me some of my abilities back so I could. He must have been okay with it."

Lana looked doubtful. "Don't forget, this is a test, Cal. He's not going to hold your hand. He may give you tools back, but not tell you how to use them."

I hadn't thought of that. My eyes glanced at the note on my desk. There was a temptation to ask my father if he agreed with removing the curse from Tiffany, but I wasn't in the mood for a lecture if he didn't. Instead, I just shrugged. "I guess all I can do is what I think is best and not worry about it."

Lana opened her mouth to say something when one of her other wards burst in to my room. It was a young girl with jet black hair and shiny orange eyes. "Strangers in the kitchen!" she yelled. "I was grabbing a snack and two people just sneaked in the back door!"

An image of Johnathan and Daniel popped into my head. I wondered if their impatience to learn about Tiffany could have brought them here.

Lana, though, seemed to draw her own conclusion. She straightened her dress, stood, and glanced once more at Tiffany. "They can't track her through The Gray, huh?" she said and hurried out of the room.

I couldn't believe the wolf pack knew she was here, but I quickly followed behind her just in case. We entered the kitchen to see Reka and Peter by the back door. They were hovering between greeting us and dashing back out the door.

"Oh, uh, hey Lana," Reka said, portraying an uncomfortable smile. "We were trying not to wake you."

"First of all, dear, I don't sleep. Secondly, we both know that's a bunch of horse puck," Lana said with a scolding tone. "Cal filled me in on your productive evening."

Reka frowned. "I thought we weren't telling people, Cal?"

I nodded. "Trust me, with what she saw, it would have been pretty hard to deny anything."

Lana crossed her arms. "Try to keep in mind, if anything happens in this house, I will find out about it." She looked at Reka. "Does your father know about any of this?"

"Are you kidding?" Peter scoffed. "If he did, we wouldn't be talking right now. He was so upset about walking in on Reka getting dressed in front of Cal; he probably wouldn't have noticed a parade in the hallway."

"Oh?" Lana looked at me, suddenly amused. "Left out a little part of the story, have we, dear?"

"No." I refused to return eye contact and hurried to change the subject. "Anyway, Tiffany is doing a lot better. The curse had not totally taken hold and I was able to draw it out. But it was close. Any longer and she probably would have been too far gone."

Peter and Reka shot surprised looks.

"That's actually pretty impressive," Peter said. "But just to be clear, you wouldn't be able to turn a full-fledged werewolf back to a human, right?"

"You mean like the two of you?" I couldn't tell if they were hopeful or worried I'd say yes. "No, I couldn't. I mean, a fully trained an—"

Lana's elbow poked sharply into my ribs.

"Uh, I mean, a fully trained being such as myself maybe could. But I'm a long way from that kind of power."

Reka narrowed her eyes. I could tell she was thinking about my gaffe, trying to figure out the broken word.

"Anyway, Tiffany is still unconscious," I said, trying to get her mind off it. "But there's a bigger problem now. What are we going to tell her when she wakes up?"

A silence fell over the small kitchen. Eyes darted between each other.

"Maybe we can just sneak her back home," Peter suggested. "Might be better to leave her with a mystery. She never saw any of us, so it's not like she can link anything to the pack."

"Except she was attacked by a wolf on your property," I said. "If anything, it'll make her more certain there are werewolves in the woods, which there are." I stroked my chin. "Although, humans have dreams, right? You think we could convince her—"

"What? That it was all a dream?" Reka pinched the bridge of her nose. "There's no way she's that stupid. Cal could say he came across her in the woods and saved her from a couple of regular wolves."

Lana laughed. "You young folk, always making things so complicated." She sat down and picked up a romance novel from the kitchen table. On the cover a young woman draped herself over a shirtless man with long hair.

"So what's your grand suggestion?" I challenged.

"Oh, sweetie. I'm not getting involved in this anymore than I already am." She cracked her book open. "Now, if you don't mind taking this into the living room so I can enjoy what little time I have to myself."

Part of me wanted to question Lana more for her advice. But she was right, it was best not to involve her any more than we already have. The three of us shuffled into the dark living room. Our faces illuminated by the light spilling out from the kitchen.

"Look, how much does this really matter anyway?" Peter asked. "I'd be pretty surprised if the council doesn't vote to do the memory wipe. So, it doesn't really matter what we tell her, does it?"

With everything that happened tonight, I had almost forgot about the whole deal with the council. "I'm still hoping we can figure out a way to convince them not to go through with it. Or maybe even protect them somehow. The Down Under might have someone that could put a protection charm on their memories or something," I mused.

Peter and Reka exchanged glances again. They came to some sort of silent agreement and Peter stepped back.

Reka took me by the shoulder. "Look, Cal, I know you've been really freaked out about the memory wipe, but Peter and I have been talking. And, well...we're not sure it's such a bad idea."

My brows furrowed. "I thought we talked about this. Didn't we agree it was too dangerous?"

"It's not just for the safety of the pack, it's for them, too." She looked over her shoulder to the stairwell, almost like she expected Tiffany to be standing there listening. "Look at tonight. Everything that happened was because those three got curious and went somewhere they had no business being. If we can take that curiosity away, they won't be as likely to do things that could get them hurt."

"But if we can explain away what happened—"

"There's nothing we can tell that girl that she won't question, and if she does, she will keep sticking her nose in it." Reka's voice grew louder and more forceful. "Before you, Peter and I never socialized at school. It's not because we didn't like the other kids." She paused and thought about it. "Well, okay, maybe that was part of it. But mostly it was because we don't want to risk exposing anything about our pack to others. It's better for them, and for us, that we remain hidden. You understand?"

Her words made sense, but I didn't want to hear them. I brushed off her hand and paced the living room. "I know what you're saying, and I'll admit, it does make sense. But things are different now. Tiffany has a target on her back. That wolf or its pack could be looking for her right now, and if she has her memory erased, she won't even know about it. That's not fair to her, is it?"

No one spoke. We had reached a stand still. I wasn't even sure anymore what I thought was right. For the first time in forever, I felt like running to my father and asking him what to do. But I knew I couldn't. As Lana reminded me tonight, *this is a test, Cal.*

"Okay, how about this?" I said at last. "It's late, and Tiffany could wake up at any time. I can bring her home and tell her parents what you suggested." I pointed at Reka. "About finding her in the woods with a couple of wolves, they'll probably take her to a hospital. Since I healed the bite, they'll just assume she passed out. When she comes to, if she starts babbling about werewolves, no one will believe her. At the very least, it will give me some time to talk to Johnathan and Daniel at school. Maybe I can convince them to stay away from your pack, maybe not. But at least it's worth a try."

Peter sighed heavily. He threw his hands up in the air. "Do what you got to do, man. I think you're wasting your time with this. My suggestion is to just let the council do the mind wipe. It's a quick and easy fix with a happy ending for everyone. But if you can't get that through your head, then go ahead, talk with them. Just know if the council decides to do the wipe, you won't be able to stop them." With that, he turned and stormed out the front door.

Reka looked torn between us, her eyes darted from the front door to me. "Don't mind him, Cal. He's just frustrated." She put a reassuring hand on my shoulder. "It doesn't mean he's wrong though." With that, she turned and headed after Peter.

I stood in the dark for a moment to gather my thoughts, but no use came of it. I headed upstairs to gather Tiffany. She still laid there asleep. I picked her up and tucked her head under my chin. Her curly hair tickled my neck. "Why did you have to complicate things?" I asked. "Couldn't you just leave well enough alone?" But of course, there was no answer. It didn't matter anyway. All I knew for certain was I was frustrated, tired, and most importantly, that I wanted to go home.

Chapter Nineteen

R^{EKA}

"I'm still having trouble believing he took the curse out of Tiffany's body," Peter said as we walked through the woods toward the house after leaving Lana's. "That's big, Reka. Really big. What is he?"

"It's huge," I said, hands raised palms up. "I have no idea what kind of creature he is, and I don't know anyone Down Under that can do that. He's half fae, but it's masked by something stronger. Still, no fairy could cure the curse, or we'd have heard about it long ago." I wrinkled my brow and concentrated on the conversation at Lana's. "Cal started to say what his father is, but Lana stopped him."

"Huh?" Peter stopped walking, grabbed my arm, and turned me toward him. "What are you talking about? I didn't hear anything that remotely hinted toward what kind of creature he is. So, when did that happen?"

"He said his mother was fae, remember? Then he started to tell us what his father was and didn't finish the word because Lana poked him in the ribs."

"Yeah, I got that much. But I thought he was reacting to the elbow punch. So, what did he say? Exactly? Like, repeat it." Peter raked both hands through dark tendrils around his face and pressed them to his temples, stormy eyes drilled holes through mine.

"Come on! I don't know exactly what he said. You had asked if he could change anybody from werewolf to human. Then he said something like, if you mean you and Reka, no. But maybe a more trained, *whatever* might be able to."

"You have to do better than *whatever*. What was the exact word he said that made you almost hear what he is?"

"That's kind of hard to figure out." My words carried a frustrated whine. "It sounded like ain."

"Aim?" Peter asked.

"No. Ain," I repeated, "It was only part of a word."

"Ain," he said softly several times, and then headed down the path again. "Okay, now we're getting somewhere. So, what kind of creature begins with A I N?"

"I don't know."

"There are so many different gods, goddesses, and elf and fae combinations it's hard to nail anything down," Peter said, then whispered, "Ain. Do you know any god's name that starts with Ain?"

"No!" I tossed my arms up. "I've been rolling that around in my brain for the last twenty minutes. I got nothing. Let me mull it over a bit more, and you can, too, because right now I want to see how Cal handles Tiffany's mother. He doesn't seem to have a clue about what's happening here."

"You don't think there's a chance in Hell he could manage to screw up our anonymity, do you?" Peter asked. "I mean, what if he insists humans should know about us? We'll all be forced to head Down Under, again. Like during the great fae war."

"You know," I said. "That may be something we should think about. If we can't tell humans who and what we are, we shouldn't be living among them."

"Okay, now you're starting to scare me." Peter choked out a laugh. "Give it a rest."

I raised an eyebrow and smiled. "Let's both chill. Cal's just a nice guy, and you know it. He saved Tiffany, told me he was half fae, and never once suggested we start parading around town with banners." I paused. "Although, Cal does look uncomfortable most of the time. He acted like he'd never had macaroni and cheese the other day, and then was all excited about a soft drink. He's definitely unsure of human behavior, and sometimes acts like living above ground is a punishment."

"Yeah, and I wondered about his father myself. Didn't you?" Peter said. "Before the whole Tiffany thing, I had no idea how powerful his dad may be."

"Yup. Many times. But think about it. We're all safe Down Under since it's neutral ground and even rogues are welcome. No questions asked. So, no matter how powerful his father is, he can't touch Down Under. My dad would probably declare us abjured from the pack if he finds out we helped Cal, anyway."

"I thought about going rogue, heading below ground, but then tried to wrap my head around the whole Gray thing. Cal pulled Tiffany in, not to mention your bed linens and bloody clothes. He took her to Lana's, too. Do you think it possible he could pull any or all of us into The Gray? That would keep your dad from finding you or Tiffany. Might be crazy to allow it. Especially since we don't know anything about, 'The Gray.'"

"Yeah, like the way out." I giggled, and Peter frowned. "Okay, so from talking with Cal, it's a place he can slip into that's somewhere between where he lives and here. It's not a magic cloak or anything like that. It's a Gray void or something. He used it at Lana's to listen to us when I asked what kind of creature Cal was.

That's when he figured out I was a wolf. So, he could be here with us right now and we wouldn't even know it."

"Swell," Peter said, walking backward and looking around. "Your bestie can have secrets, but we aren't allowed to have any. I'm going to ask him some serious questions."

"Not until after this weekend's pack meeting!" I had tossed around something that could nail down a decision about my future. If I was right, it would change a lot of things. "We both should definitely know more then."

"You don't plan on telling your father at the meeting, do you?" Peter's eyes widened and his jaw dropped.

"Don't be such a smart butt. This is serious. Of course not. I'm going to test my father's love for me. And don't ask how. You'll just have to wait and see."

"Don't do anything stupid," he said.

"Shut up! Get back on track." I wasn't going to let him push me for answers with Dad and the meeting. "Cal? Remember? What is he? I think it's about time I find out. I can't be loyal to someone who avoids giving up his nature. It shows no trust in me."

"Not like I haven't been telling you that for the past few days."

Snap! I knew that would sidetrack him. "I know," I said, and lowered my eyes like a good submissive female wolf. Hated it.

"How much further are you going to take this Cal thing? We've got a big situation. Tiffany's been bit by a wolf from *another pack* on *our* property. And if that isn't enough to wig your father out, your pal, Cal, pulled the infection from the bite right out of her body. Now that's freaking epic. When are you going to give that up?"

Crap! That didn't last long. I winged it. "That is *so not* as important as finding out what Tiffany knows first. And if Cal actually did heal her."

BY THE TIME WE GOT to Tiffany's house, Cal was waving goodbye as the family car backed out of the driveway.

"Do you think we should say something to him? Ask if it went well?" I asked Peter while watching Cal smile at Tiffany's shadowed face behind the car's window.

"No," Peter quickly answered. "He looks fine. He's smiling for heaven's sake. We came here to see how he handled the whole thing, and we would've been able to hear whatever he said from right here, but that's not an option now. I guess he can move pretty quick in that Gray area, huh?"

"Looks like it. I hope he didn't say anything that can get all of us in trouble. I know he means well. But I also know he's in learning mode and knows very little about Otherworld creatures. He said as much at Lana's. So whatever type of creature or combo of creatures he is, he hasn't got a total handle on it."

Peter snickered. "Not any different from any of us his age—unless you've got the alpha-werewolf-I'm-just-as-good-as-any-man thing nailed down—and like you said, we're not one hundred percent sure he *did* pull the virus from Tiffany."

Crap. What a butt wipe. And I thought I did have the alpha thing nailed down. He'd find out after tomorrow's meeting. "Do you always have to be such an ass?"

"I strive to live up to your standards."

I sighed loudly. "So, what now? The hospital?"

"I don't think so. They'd probably have to hit the ER. The place is always a zoo. I wonder if we can see her after they get home and before we go to school tomorrow. Sometime within the next ten hours, we need to have a talk with Tiffany. And we *do* need to keep Cal in the loop."

I smiled up at Peter. "That last sentence was pivotal, man. Pivotal."

A HAND COVERED MY MOUTH and woke me from a sound sleep. Before I could focus or phase into a wolf, Peter's voice hushed me. It seemed like I'd just fallen asleep seconds ago. He removed his hand and I let out a frustrated yawn.

"What time is it? It's still dark outside." I sounded grumpy, so I cleared my throat and softly asked, "Everything okay?"

"Yes, but it won't be if you don't get up quietly, get dressed, grab your books, and let's get going."

Peter tugged the covers off me, grabbed my hand, pulled me out of bed, and pointed me in the direction of my dresser. "I want to get to Tiffany's early so we can wake her before her parents get up. I think we can climb the roof under her bedroom window."

"Yeah, all that sounds good," I said and pulled a black long-sleeved tee over my head after fastening my bra. I shed my pajama bottoms for a pair of jeans and slipped into socks and my tennis shoes, the brief nudity no more an issue than a sneeze. "But what if Tiffany goes all rabid crazy on us and starts screaming her brains out?"

I walked across the bedroom, finger-combing my hair, and Peter pushed my backpack into my chest. I hoisted it over my shoulder, and he pulled up the bedroom window.

Ten minutes later, we stood under Tiffany's bedroom window. The house was dark, so we climbed a honeysuckle trellis to an oak tree with branches stretched across the metal rooftop. I suddenly had a horrid thought we'd have to tap on Tiffany's window, but it was open about six inches—stupid with a stray wolf out searching her scent. I made a mental note to address that.

We stood on either side of her bed, both of us probably thinking the same thing. This could get pretty ugly if we woke her parents. Not to mention, she already thought we were wolves, and probably thought it was one of us that bit her. Before I could tell Peter my concerns, he clamped his hand over her mouth just like he did mine. Tiffany immediately screamed under it—I had no idea how loud a muffled scream could be.

"Well, now, that was stupid," I hissed at Peter and then bent down close to her ear. "Tiffany, stay calm. You're gonna wake your mother and father. We are not here to hurt you. We're here to protect you. No one from our pack bit you. It was a stray werewolf."

Peter looked horrified, and at the same time, wore a *what the heck* expression.

Tiffany immediately quieted down but crab-walked backward until her shoulders were up against the headboard, heels still pushing. "I'm not going to school today," she said with a shaky voice. "So, you don't have to worry about me telling anybody anything. Cal came over and tried to make me believe that he saw me in the woods with a wolf and you saved me. A plain old wolf, not a werewolf like you two. You and I both know what he said isn't true."

Tiffany pulled her comforter—a lacy pink-flowered, prissy thing—up around her neck. "I don't believe you, either, Reka. I don't know which one of you bit me, but that wasn't very nice."

She stuck her foot out from under the comforter and tugged it up to her knee. "And how did the bite disappear? I know I'm not crazy because there's a mole in the shape of a paw print above my ankle where the bite was." Tiffany pointed to the wolf's mark. "See it? Don't even try to tell me you don't," she angrily whispered. "Talk about freaky. If you don't tell me the whole truth, I'll just find out, anyway. And Jonathan and Daniel are not going to be very happy when I tell them Cal has been lying to us. He is not human either. Am I right?"

"Alright, Tiffany, calm down," Peter said. "Nobody bit you. And the wolf you saw was not...a werewolf. Cal was telling you—"

"Nip it right there!" Tiffany hissed. "Reka just said a wolf bit me, alright, and not one from your pack. Do you think I'm deaf? Because I am not as dumb as I look. You don't just get bit by a werewolf and forget it. It's freaking epic!"

Peter hushed her. I pushed Peter aside. "Okay, here's the thing. Cal did find you, and he carried you to my house to tell me you'd been bit by a wolf. I told him it was not one of us." I stood there and watched her eyes grow while I listened to Peter's short breaths as he paced around the bedroom.

"Swell," Peter mumbled. "She not only got bit, she knows we're shifters. And she bares the mark of her biter."

"I do? I knew it. Am I going to turn into a werewolf? I hope not, because I won't go around growling and barking in public like a dog. And I refuse to pee in the woods."

I snorted. I couldn't help it. Peter frowned at me.

"No, Tiffany. We don't think you are going to turn," Peter said. "It seems Cal took you to the boarding house and somehow healed you from the infection that the bite gave you. You may not have lived through the infection. Not many do. So, he saved your life.

We won't know for sure until the next full moon, but you could feel some changes in the next twenty-four hours, too. Heightened sight, smell, and strength."

Tiffany yelped. "I'm not going to get muscles or hair on my chest, or anything crazy like that, am I?"

"Do I look like a guy?" I asked. *If she says yes, I'm going to die.*

"No," she spat. "Why are you here? And why are you telling me all this?" Tiffany's eyelids narrowed.

"Yeah, go ahead, smarty," Peter said to me. "I want to hear this, too. Let's just give it all up to a blonde—"

"Don't you even, Peter Westgate!" I took a deep breath and turned to Tiffany. "Look, you. That paw print mole you just showed us. It's his mark you're wearing. So, even if you don't change, he owns you."

"Get out! No one owns me. Not even me," Tiffany said and tucked the comforter tightly around her calf.

I wanted to shake my head but, instead, looked at Peter. It was like a light turned on behind his eyelids. His jaw dropped, and he sighed. "Swell, he doesn't have to go looking for her. He can track her. The wolf that bit you will find you, Tiffany, and if he's part of a pack, they can find you, too."

Tiffany looked terrified. She was surrounded in pink. Her hair laid on a pink t-shirt, and one exposed knee was covered in gray and pink plaid. Tendrils of dreamy blonde hair fell sensuously over her face. Nothing like my morning face and bedhead hair. Her blue eyes sparkled in the moonlight. And she clutched the comforter with long fingernails painted light pink. The toenails on the foot she had slid out from under the covers matched her fingernails. She would have probably made a beautiful wolf. *If she lived through it.*

I sat on the edge of the bed. Tiffany's breaths were short and pushed. Her forehead was shiny with sweat. She moved her legs over to give me room.

"I'm sorry this happened to you. I'm sure we were not the only wolfpack that knew you and Jonathan and Daniel, were getting closer to finding out that we existed. Unfortunately, we have no idea who the wolf is. So, the only thing we can do is protect you from him."

"And how do you plan to do that?" Tiffany said, her shoulders stiff.

She smelled like a wounded animal. That scent would add to the wolf's ability to find her.

"I'm going to become your new best friend," I said.

Tiffany's eyes turned to shock mode again. Then she slid out from under the covers, grabbed a pink robe off the headboard post, and pulled it on. I was prepared for an argument.

"Don't worry," I quickly said. "I'm not crazy about this either, but it's totally necessary that we—"

"Really? A bestie?" Tiffany squealed. "I've never had a real best girlfriend." She cinched the robe and strutted past me. "I think I'm going to school today. Help me pick out something to wear, will ya, Reka?"

Double Crap!

I glared at Peter's grin. If he laughed, I was going to bite him.

Chapter Twenty

C ALASTAIR

The next morning, I arrived at school early, hoping to talk with Johnathan and Daniel before classes started. With any luck, I'd catch them before they heard about Tiffany. I waited outside the front door, soaking in the cool fall air. An occasional student walked by, taking little notice of me. Either tapping away on their cell phone or chatting with a friend.

Finally, I saw Johnathan making his way down the sidewalk. It was the first time I could recall seeing him on his own. As he noticed me waiting, his long strides turned into marches.

"Hey, copper top!" he shouted. His normally playful nickname for me had a biting tone today. A swirl of colorful leaves blew past him as he approached. "What the hell, man? You were going to text me when you found Tiffany, but ya never did. Then this morning I hear from her in the hospital?! What's the deal?"

I was disappointed to hear he had already talked to Tiffany. Hopefully, she hadn't told him too much. "Sorry, John. I meant to, but I couldn't figure out Tiffany's phone password, and I don't have your number...or a phone for that matter."

His expression lightened a little. "Well...alright, I guess. I was up half the night wondering what was going on. Didn't hear much from Tiff. She was still pretty tired. What went down out there?"

Here we go, time to tap into my fae lying skills. "Man, you guys really shouldn't go out in those woods anymore, especially at night," I said, trying not to sound rehearsed. "There's some crazy animals around here. I had to scare off a couple wolves to get Tiffany out of there. I didn't see any wounds on her, though. Figured she fainted or hit her head on a rock or something."

Johnathan's ears perked up at the mention of wolves. "What kind of wolves? Where they big or seem stronger than normal?"

I crossed my arms. "Do you mean, were they werewolves?"

"What? No. I didn't mean..." Johnathan frantically backtracked. "No one said anything about werewolves. I'm just...curious about the wildlife in the woods." He looked embarrassed by my question. As if hearing the word werewolf out loud suddenly sounded silly.

"Don't BS me, Johnathan. I know why you guys have been asking me about Reka and her family. I've heard the rumors around school. That's why Tiffany was on their property last night, wasn't it? Looking for clues that the family is under some kind of curse?" I paused for an answer that never came. "Hate to break it to ya, but they're just a regular family that likes to keep to themselves. Imagine it probably doesn't help they hide out in a cabin in the woods, I'll admit. But still, they're nothing but eccentric."

Johnathan scuffed one of his blue and black tennis shoes against the other. "Look," he said sheepishly. "I know how it sounds. Really, I do. I didn't believe the rumors for a long time. It just seemed like one of those urban legends kids like to tell to make fun of people who are a little...different, ya know? But then...I, um..." With great effort, Johnathan made eye contact with me. "Dude, look, ya got to keep this to yourself, okay? You can't tell Reka or I'll die."

I nodded, intrigued as to where this was going.

"Well, in junior high I had quite the crush on Reka." His cheeks reddened; under other circumstances, it could have been humorous. "I just never had the guts to say anything to her. Not like it would have been easy anyway, always on her own or hanging out with Peter, who's not exactly the most approachable person either. But I really wanted to invite her to the winter homecoming dance. So, I thought it might be easier to ask her at her home, ya know, away from the other kids in the class, just so if she said no it wouldn't be as embarrassing. Well, I was walking down the road, trying to gather my nerves when I saw a wolf come barging out the front door of their house. I ducked into the woods before it could see me. A second later, a man walked out the door, too. He didn't seem rattled like you'd think if a wild animal had just been in the house. I wasn't close enough to see much. The whole thing just seemed, odd."

That was more solid evidence than I was hoping he had, but it could be explained away. "Well, from what I've seen, they are pretty into nature. It's possible the wolf just lived around the area and they let it come in once and a while, like a pet. Doesn't prove that anyone in the house is shedding their human skin and turning into wolves."

"I know, I know. But it was just an odd coincidence after hearing all the rumors for so long. When I told Daniel and Tiffany about it, they wanted to investigate. It just started out as kind of a fun activity, not anything we took too seriously. But the more stories we heard, the more we began to wonder if there was some truth to it all."

Johnathan was much more rational than I thought. I realized it was possible to convince him to let this whole thing go just by compelling his logical side. My mind already began spinning ideas when I saw Daniel walking down the sidewalk towards us.

"Hey," Johnathan said casually, expecting him to automatically join us.

But Daniel just gave a light head bob and continued toward the door.

Johnathan turned to face him, trying to get his attention. "Yo Daniel, what's up?"

"Nothing," Daniel replied dismissively. Without even so much as looking at us, he entered the school.

Johnathan frowned and turned back to me. "Huh, that's weird."

"You two get into a fight or something last night after I saw you?" I asked.

"No. We walked home, sent a few texts later, mostly about Tiffany. He seemed fine, though. Just worried about her after we didn't hear from you. Thought he'd be eager to hear what happened." Johnathan stood there a moment thinking before hurrying after Daniel.

I followed close by. If something was going on with these two, I needed to know. We caught up with him by his locker. He barely acknowledged us as we approached.

"Hey, you pissed or something?" Johnathan asked.

Daniel looked more confused by the question than anything. "No, why?"

"You kind of blew us off back there. You and I always hang out before school."

Daniel shrugged. "Sorry. I guess I'm just focused on classes. I'm here to learn, not chit chat ya know."

Johnathan was taken aback. "Okay...aren't you at least curious about Tiffany?"

"What about her?"

Johnathan's frustration boiled over. "She's in the hospital, Dan! We spent a good portion of last night worrying whether Cal could—"

"Who's Cal?" Daniel interrupted.

A shiver ran down my spine.

The question gave Johnathan pause before gesturing at me. Daniel looked at me, but I saw no hint of recognition in his eyes. They seemed hollow somehow, lacking the emotion I'd become used to from him. I scanned him with my empathic abilities and found none of the passion I sensed before that used to drive his curiosity and loyalty to his friends. He seemed more like a husk, with little on the inside.

"Don't you remember?" Johnathan persisted. "We met up last night, Cal was going to look for Tiff because she was running late." Getting no response, he continued. "She was in the woods, ya know," he hushed his voice, "trying to figure out if Reka's family were werewolves?"

Daniel's eyes glossed over at the mention of werewolves. "For crying out loud, we're in high school. Grow up." He shut his locker and zipped his pine green backpack. "I'm going to get to class early. You guys just go do whatever you're doing and leave me out of it. I got better things to worry about." With that, he turned and walked away.

Johnathan looked as if he was just punched in the gut. "We've been friends since first grade," he reminisced. "I've never seen him like that. Sure, he can have a bit of a temper, but he acted like he hardly knew me. It's like he woke up as an entirely different person."

"Yeah," I said, half-heartedly. It wasn't a mystery to me what had happened. I could tell from the moment Daniel's blank eyes looked into mine. The council must have already voted and decided to wipe their memories. And Daniel was their first victim.

The effects were greater than I anticipated. I had worried about collateral damage if they removed memories that made a person who they were. But in Daniel's case, it seemed to affect his whole personality. Whatever wonder and curiosity used to be there was gone. Without it, his passion for friends had suffered, and he no longer seemed to care about them, even a long term one like Johnathan.

Removing the three of their memories almost seemed like a good idea last night. Peter thought it was a quick fix with no downside. But seeing what it did to Daniel, how it changed who he was to his core. I couldn't let it go on. I may have been too late for Daniel, but maybe I could still help the other two.

"Look, Johnathan. We need to talk."

JOHNATHAN WAS STILL upset from his conversation with Daniel. His tall, lanky frame hunched over with a defeated posture. But he waited patiently for me to speak.

I wasn't confident this was the best time to do a one eighty on our previous conversation and tell him the truth about what was going on, but it wasn't really up to me. If the vampires conducted the memory wipe on Daniel, they'd soon be coming for the other two in his group. I dragged Johnathan into a nearby empty classroom, so no one would overhear us.

"Okay, look. This isn't really my place to tell you, but under the circumstances, there isn't much choice." I paused, hesitant to continue. "But you're right, there are werewolves in the woods."

Johnathan's expression remained still. He stared doubtfully at me. "But you just said there wasn't..."

"I know. Forget all that. I was trying to get you to leave this alone. It was attracting too much attention from the wrong people. I thought if I could convince you there was nothing out of the ordinary in the woods, maybe the whole thing would blow over. But I don't think that's the case."

Johnathan put his hands on his hips and looked down at me. "Are you telling me the truth, or trying to make fun of me or something?"

A group of students wandered past, voices and laughter muffled with curiosity. I instinctively lowered my voice. "It's true. I shouldn't be telling you this for...just, so many reasons. I'm actually not sure why I am..."

Wait, why am I? I'm Reka's guardian angel, not his. But I've spent so much time on earth worrying about these three. A guardian is given the responsibility of one person, and not entitled to interfere with others. And by doing so I've put myself at risk of failing the test. So, what the hell am I doing?

"I guess, I don't know, I never really fit in where I came from." I moved further from the passing students and Johnathan followed. "Everybody thought I was strange, and a trouble maker. In a lot of ways, they were right. I believed things that the others didn't share, and always felt separate and alone because of it. Then I saw you, Tiffany, and Daniel were the same way, but it didn't seem to bother you guys. You just did your own thing, and, to be honest, that kind of annoyed me at first. But now, I guess I kind of admire it. And there are things going on here that I don't agree with. I just can't sit back and let it happen, even if it technically isn't 'my place' to intervene. So, yes, there are werewolves, and other creatures, too, roaming around the world. It's better you know that than being left in the dark."

Johnathan stood there for an uncomfortably long time with a stony expression. "I knew it!" he abruptly exploded. "Everyone thought I was crazy! But I knew something was going on! Hold on, I'll go find Daniel, so you can tell him all that over again."

Johnathan scampered toward a side door by the auditorium. I quickly lunged and threw my arm across the door to prevent him from opening it.

"Hey, you don't get it, do you!" I said. "These are dangerous people who don't want a bunch of teenagers running around blabbing about their secrets."

"Exactly. They *are* dangerous," he countered. "Don't the people around here have the right to know about them?"

Good point.

I crossed my arms and leaned against the door. "Alright but let me ask you this. Let's say you start telling people about all this, and that somehow, they believe you. What comes next?"

Johnathan's brow furrowed.

"Do you think everyone is going to accept them for who they are?" I continued. "The human race doesn't exactly have a history of excepting people who are different, do they?"

Johnathan scoffed. "This isn't like a different religion or skin color. These are monsters that are living next door to us"

"Oh, is that right?" I struggled not to take offense from the stereotype, seeing as I was one of these supernatural beings myself. "Let me tell ya something, bud. Of everyone I've met since I've come here, there's no one I trust more than Reka. She's been working behind the scenes to help you three stay out of danger. She's even the one who saved Tiffany last night in the woods. And all you guys do is try to expose her personal information to the public."

Johnathan lowered his eyes.

"Okay, look, John. I didn't tell you all this so you could go spreading it around town. It's important you understand that you three have ruffled some feathers with all the poking around you've done. Many of these creatures are very secretive about who they are because they worry what would happen if they were exposed. There's a council made up of different beings across Michigan. They've seen what you've been up to and are worried you could bring them to light. So, they decided the best way to keep you from finding the truth was to...well, wipe your memory of the werewolves."

The color drained from his face. "Can they really do that?"

"Actually, I think they already have. The way Daniel's been acting makes me pretty sure they've already gotten to him."

Johnathan took a step back and ran his fingers through his hair. "You serious? So, Daniel...he doesn't..." He started pacing the room. "He doesn't remember our investigating the woods, so without those memories, it's changed his personality."

"Erasing those memories took away his open-mindedness and ability to question reality. Without it, he's lost his sense of adventure." I watched Johnathan as he walked back and forth. I was sympathetic; it was a lot of information to absorb in a short time. But we couldn't stand here all day. "Come on, we got to find Tiffany."

"What about Daniel? Can we do anything to get his memory back? Like, hypnosis or something?"

Behind Johnathan's hazel eyes, I saw hope. His concern was admirable, and I wished I could have told him what he wanted to hear.

"I'm sorry, but hypnosis only helps with memories that are buried. His are actually erased. There's no way to bring them back. The only thing we can do now is keep you two from having your memories taken as well."

Johnathan hung his head. "Alright. I guess we should find out if Tiffany is here today. I hope they haven't gotten to her, too."

Chapter Twenty-One

R^{EKA} "Now, remember, as much as you might want to, you can't tell Daniel and Johnathan anything about getting bit by a shifter. Got it?"

"They've been my best friends since, like, forever, and they will know," Tiffany said as we headed through town toward the high school.

"How will they know? You don't look like you've been attacked," Peter said. "There aren't any wolf bites or scratches on you. Are you connected through some telepathic thing?"

"No. Not technically. But Johnathan is kind of weird. Like he knows what I'm thinking before I think it." Tiffany flipped her blonde curls behind her shoulder. "He does the same thing with Daniel. You'll see if you hang with us."

Her eyes popped with the powder blue sweater she wore, and skinny jeans made her legs look long. My left eye twitched and I tried to calm it with my fingers. I so did not want to hang with Tiffany or her friends. I looked frumpy beside her, and it made me think I needed to put some color on my cheeks, shade my eye lids, and fluff my hair a bit. I looked down at my low slung 501 Levi's and long-sleeved tee. *Crap!* I felt better in guy clothes. My hips were too small, and my waist was not.

"Fine, but you can't say werewolf," I said. "And you have to promise. If you do, you'll be putting them in danger." I tried to wipe a hopeful look off my face and slap on a death-wish gaze. I don't think it was working.

Peter inhumanly growled, grabbed Tiffany by the arm, and swung her around to face him. "Look at me. Do I look like the boy next door?" His eyes flashed gold. "Because I'm trying really hard to warn you without taking a bite out of you myself. If you tell a human, any human, it won't only be me playing big bad wolf. You were lucky. Reka saved you and Cal fixed you. Damn lucky. But your friends could get bit and turn or even die if you get them stirred up.

"You've been marked. Other wolves will smell that, sense it. That will never change. But it can be a good thing because with that mark comes a certain amount of respect, support, and protection. But if you break that trust, it's over."

Tiffany stared at Peter. Her eyes big, her mouth half open. *Crap.* She looked even cuter.

I threw my arms up. "Okay, let's not freak her out before we educate her. Properly. Tiffany needs to meet Dad. The pack may help her understand."

"Now you're talking," Peter said. "And we have a meeting tomorrow."

"Are you kidding? Me and a pack of werewolves, and...what?" Tiffany did an about-face. "Suddenly, I think going to school is a bad idea. I've been bitten by a wolf. I may or may not turn into a big smelly animal that wants to eat helpless animals—try to live with that hanging that over your head. I binge watched *Teen Wolf* with Daniel and Johnathan! I know what to expect."

Tiffany shuddered and then threw up on the ground. I noticed she was careful to miss her shoes. She pulled a tissue from her pocket and dabbed at her lips, then glared at me.

"You're supposed to protect me, not terrorize me!" Tiffany said. "Instead, you threaten me with endangering my two best friends in the world, and then drop the 'I'm part of your pack' thing." The dainty hands with painted fingernails flew up again. "This is too much."

"Too much?" I wanted to hit something. "Suck it up, miss-prom-queen-wannabe. No one told you to trespass on to our property—at night, no less—to spy on us. Wake up and toss away your little red hood. This is no fairytale. You screwed up. Don't be the one to bring it down around your friends' heads. Hopefully, we can stop it, and you'll be the only causality."

Tiffany puffed air out her nose—even that was ladylike—and then she pouted. Her bottom lip actually puffed out before she hugged her backpack and started to walk back the way we came.

"Besides," Tiffany whined, "I can't keep secrets. I told Melanie Daniels she was going to be prom queen last year after the ballots were counted. Remember?" She tossed a glance over her shoulder as we followed. "Maybe not. You didn't even go to prom."

No way I was hitting a room full of giggling girls in frilly dresses accompanied by testosterone wacked out guys. Mother Earth be damned! I'd be cutting myself again if I had to hang with this chick much longer.

"It was senior prom," I said, putting the emphasis on the word senior. "I wasn't a senior."

"Didn't matter. You could have gone. All you had to do was get asked." Tiffany sounded smug as she gracefully jogged across a street and on to a dirt road. "I was asked, three times, and I was also on the decorating committee."

"Of course you were," I said, the early morning sun glaring in my eyes. I hooded them with my hand and kept pace, "and who wants to decorate? Not me!" *Blessed be the full moon! I want to strangle her.*

Tiffany shouted. "Stop undermining my choices! If you want to become my friend, then act like it! I am who I am. And you are what you are. I'd rather be me before the bite and then you wouldn't have to try." She turned to the wolf on her other side and shouted. "You're right, Peter. Okay? I screwed up! I went were I shouldn't have! And I got bit by a werewolf!"

Tiffany's hand went right to her mouth. "See what I mean?" she said around her fingers "My mouth works faster than my brain. It's a good thing we're skipping school today. And sorry you have to be my friend. Both of you. You don't really have a choice, do you?" She covered her face and burst into tears.

Crap.

I patted Tiffany's arm as I jogged beside her. "We can do this. We *will* be friends. That's all that matters. The pack will help get this resolved." I sucked at the comforting sympathy thing.

"Like I want to be in the middle of a pack of wolves. Ohmigod!" Tiffany screeched. "I could be a wolf!"

Double crap.

Chapter Twenty-Two

CALASTAIR

Johnathan and I searched the school, looking for Tiffany. We peeked into her first hour class and didn't see her, and she wasn't in the hall by her locker. We even waited outside the women's bathroom, but all that got us was strange looks from our other classmates.

"Maybe she stayed home," Johnathan suggested. "I mean...if I went through what she did last night, I would."

"You're probably right. We should check her house."

The 5-minute bell rang. Johnathan's eyes shifted down the hall. "We're not supposed to leave school after it starts."

"Under the circumstances, I think it's okay," I said impatiently. I grabbed his arm and pulled him toward the exit.

Mrs. Mackle poked her head out of the classroom. "Hey, where are you two going?"

I drove my elbow into the door bar. "We're leaving. Don't blame Johnathan. I'm a bad influence."

We headed over to Tiffany's house. Both cars were gone, and no one answered when we knocked.

"Maybe she's still asleep," Johnathan offered. "She's not much of a morning person."

I tested the doorknob. It was locked. "Well, I guess there's one way to make sure. Do you know which room hers is?

"Yeah, it's around back."

"Show me."

We hopped over the chain link gate to their backyard. Off in the distance, I heard a lawn mower start up. I hoped whoever it was wouldn't spot us sneaking around.

"Alright. Which one?" I asked, scanning the back of their house.

Johnathan hesitantly pointed to a window on the second floor, toward the right side of the house. "You sure?"

"Pretty sure. Look, I only saw her room once. Tiffany's parents didn't like us going in there because, well you know...they didn't think it was appropriate."

I couldn't help but roll my eyes. Beneath her window were a couple of garbage cans. Perfect. I adjusted them a little to make sure they sat on stable ground. "Okay, hop on," I said, slapping the top of the can. It clanged as the lid snapped shut.

Johnathan frowned. "What?"

"I need you to peek in the window, see if she is in there."

"Why me? I mean, this is your idea and all."

"I'm not tall enough to reach the ledge, and I'm not jumping up and down on one of these things."

Johnathan glanced up at the window. "I don't...what if, you know, she's in there getting dressed or something."

His cheeks reddened. I could tell he was trying not to picture it.

"What if she's in there having her memory wiped by a bunch of vampires," I said, again tapping the lid of the can. "Get on up there."

With my help, Johnathan climbed on the wobbly can. He gingerly pulled himself up and peered inside Tiffany's window. Placing his hands on either side of his face to block out the sun, he scanned the room before hopping down. "That was her room, but I didn't see her in there."

"Damnit!" I kicked a nearby rock into the thick green grass.

"Maybe she got to school after we left. It wouldn't be the first time she showed up late."

That was possible, but then it was also possible her parents took her back to the hospital, or to animal control to tell them about the crazy wolves in the woods, or she could just be wandering aimlessly around town. I had hoped I wouldn't have to track her through all of Reed City. But if I had to, the fastest way would be to travel through The Gray. But I couldn't do that with Johnathan in tow.

"Look, man. This is turning out to be more of a hassle than I thought. I think it would be safer to drop you off at Lana's and then keep searching by myself."

"Wouldn't it be better if I hung around the police station or something?"

Poor fool; he doesn't understand the power that was after him. "When it comes to this, the safest place in town is Lana's. It's just, too complicated to explain why. You'll have to trust me on this one."

Johnathan looked unsure but agreed.

Chapter Twenty-Three

<u>REKA</u>

"Do you hear the other voices?" I pressed.

"What other voices?" Tiffany pulled at a tendril of hair and stuffed it into the corner of her mouth.

"The other voices in your head?" Peter puffed frustration.

"Huh?" Tiffany said. "By the way, Mr. You, I'm not afraid."

"That's nice," Peter sighed. "Can we get back to the questioning voices?"

"Who said anything about questioning? Are you reading my mind now? I just wish everyone would get out of *my* mind." She narrowed her eyes. "So, there are voices. Not questioning. Scolding. But I try not to listen."

"You need to start listening!" Peter shouted.

Tiffany jumped with a yelp.

"You're a skittery pup," Peter said. "Unless you're wandering a wooded area at night where you believe werewolves live. What the heck?"

"I'd be scared, too, Peter. Now back off," I said. "Tiff, I know it's hard, but we're trying to protect you, hon. So, if the voices in your head start talking, take notes, okay?"

"I don't have a pencil and paper, Reka."

"Can you take mental notes?" Peter asked quietly and hopefully.

I choked back a laugh. At least he tried. "How about you get our attention the next time you hear or feel him. Maybe telling us as he talks will help?"

"Hey, I just thought of something," Tiffany said.

"What?" Peter and I responded at once.

"What if the wolf was a girl?" Tiffany blushed. "I mean, I didn't look or anything. Big teeth and growls kind of nipped any exploration, ya know? The wolf's eyes were yellow, though. If that helps."

Peter rumbled again.

"Tiff, when you hear him, uh, them, are they guy voices or girl?"

"Ah, dah," Tiffany said as she slapped her forehead with her palm. "Guys. They're all guys."

"All?" Peter and I asked. "Did you hear—"

"Reka! Peter! Is that Tiffany with you?" my father shouted from the porch one hundred yards away.

He didn't look pleased.

Crap.

"Hey, Daddy." I waved. "We have a problem."

Dad crossed his arms over his chest. "Lana called."

Double crap.

Chapter Twenty-four

<u>CALASTAIR</u>

When we got to Lana's, I gently opened the door. Thankfully, we seemed to arrive during one of the quiet times in the house. I could hear children playing upstairs in their rooms, but there was no sign of Lana. Which was good, considering her objections to interfering with the werewolf curse. I imagined there would be a similar argument about the vampires. We stepped inside silently and I walked to the stairs and glanced up.

"Okay, we should be good," I whispered. "Head upstairs and my room is the third door on the right. I'll be back after I find Tiffany."

Johnathan walked up the stairs and disappeared from view. The shag carpeting of the hallway muffled his footsteps. I smiled to myself. Something had finally gone right. Till I turned around and found Lana standing behind me, arms crossed, and she wore a scorn wrinkled expression. Her sudden appearance almost sent me sprawling backward on the staircase.

"What are you, part boogie man or something?" I asked. "Do you always stalk around the house?!"

"I could ask you the same thing," she said calmly. "Especially since you're here on a school day with Johnathan."

"Oh," I said defeated. "You know he's here, too, huh?"

"I told you before, Cal, nothing happens in this house without me finding out. I know you wouldn't be sneaking around if you two were just playing hooky. Now spill."

I was going to ask what kind of game 'hooky' was but decided it didn't matter.

"Alright, long story short, a group of vampires are looking for Johnathan and his friends to wipe their memories, and I figured I'd leave him here to keep him safe while I look for his other friend."

Lana's expression remained stone cold.

"And, yes," I said, "I do realize we just talked about this kind of thing the other night, but I'm not asking you to intervene. I'm just hoping the vampires wouldn't want to trespass onto neutral territory. We could just say Johnathan came over to play a game of hooky or something."

Lana sighed. "That sounds like a slippery slope, Cal, and vampires aren't dumb."

I scratched my head and looked down at my shoes. "Look, I'm not trying to put you in any kind of danger or anything—"

Lana laughed. "Oh, sweetie, if you think I couldn't handle a couple of vampires, then you don't know much about me. I'm not afraid of them. It's a matter of house rules."

I remained silent to let Lana ponder her next words.

She scoffed. "Alright. Johnathan can stay here for now, but only because you have something more important to do."

Getting the answer I wanted, I quickly headed toward the front door as to not push my luck. "Thanks, Lana. I'll make it up to you!"

"Wait! Stop! That's not what I meant," she called after me before I could step out the door.

"I thought you said..."

"I said there was something important, not to run out looking for Johnathan's friend." She pointed toward the back door in the kitchen. "Your father is waiting for you in the yard."

Chapter Twenty-Five

<u>REKA</u>

Some of the pack sat around our kitchen table, others surrounded us on two or four feet. Tiffany was between Peter and me, wide-eyed and her hands were shaking.

"When was the last time any of you ate?" Tiffany asked. "Just saying. You all look hungry."

One side of Raz's mouth quivered upward. "We don't eat humans, Tiffany. We hunt our property for wildlife, much like your camouflaged neighbors hunt theirs, only without guns or bows. But we also shop at the grocery. I had eggs, bacon, and biscuits for breakfast."

"Are you hungry?" Peter asked Tiffany. "We kind of snagged you from your bedroom before the sun came up this morning. I smell bacon. Would you like some?"

"If I eat right now, I'll puke," Tiffany said. "I'm really sorry about all the problems I've caused, Mr. Cassady, but I just had to know what you guys were. I mean, if you were wolves. You know."

"It's not your fault they are who they are," Zrinka said, and pulled a basket of biscuits from the oven. "I kept these warm for Peter and Reka. Why don't you have one with them?"

"I heard Reka had a sister," Tiffany said. "You said *they* are who *they* are. Are you really her sister? Are you being held captive?"

My father snarled.

"I'm Reka's twin sister, but I don't shift," Zrinka smiled. "I've been home schooled all my life. And when I had a choice, I chose not to go to school. It's safer for the pack."

"Everyone else had breakfast." Lola jumped up of the floor where she'd been sitting next to her husband, Bogdan, who was in wolf form. "I could scramble up some eggs and warm the leftover bacon. Peter, Reka?"

"I could eat," Peter said. "It's been a long night."

Lola Longue, a gamma wolf shifter was adopted by humans, and only sixteen when Bogdan met her at the local veterinary clinic where she cleaned kennels. He had brought Buddy in for his shots, and Lola was stocking shelves behind the desk. She joined the pack when Bogdan married her a week after she turned eighteen.

Dad was simmering like a kettle about to whistle.

"Reka?" Lola pushed.

"No thanks." I could not believe Peter wanted to eat. My stomach was rumbling, but it wasn't for food.

Dad hadn't taken his eyes off me since we all sat down. They were rimmed in gold. Not like they weren't that way most of the time lately when he was around me. He has been so hostile with me. Like when Peter, Tiffany, and I walked into the house earlier, the whole pack was in the living room except my father. After he made the Lana comment, he had abruptly turned and walked back into the house. Papo, Adelina, and Raz had ushered everyone into the kitchen and Dad was at the table waiting, eyes glowing. I sat across from my father and Raz sat beside him. He had lowered his eyes and turned his head away from my father but laid his arm against Dad's. My father's eyes dilated and shrunk the gold.

"Tiffany says she can hear the wolf that bit her." I spoke first. "But I don't think she's going to turn because Cal was able to pull the wolf virus from her body with the help of his father."

I swallowed hard and took a deep breath when my father's jaw tightened, and he moved his head from side to side, bones cracking up his spine. He was fighting the change—Raz kept him at bay by being close, arms touching.

"I would've told you, Dad, but when Cal said he could fix this, I didn't want to start a war with another pack. You know how you get. But then decided you needed to know regardless. So we pulled Tiffany from her bedroom and brought her here."

That got his attention.

My father slammed his fists on the table. "You have stepped over a line, Reka, of which you can never return."

"See," I said. "You can't even discuss this like a pack leader. I'm your daughter, and with that comes a certain amount of responsibility. I felt my decision to wait until tomorrow's meeting more beneficial for the pack."

With a deep and guttural voice, Dad said, "You don't make decisions for my pack! You would have allowed over twelve hours to go by before we could send out scouts to follow a scent. Thank those wise and mature in our world; Lana called. Hopefully, we will find the intruder and tend to the safety of Tiffany until next full moon."

Dad raked his fingernails across the table and left eight jagged lines. "You are not pack leader, Reka! Nothing about you being my daughter gives you the right to decide anything for our benefit. You played out a little fantasy. Let your new friend—one no one knows anything of substance about—take a newly bit human and perform...whatever, hoping she will not turn on the next full moon."

"But it worked! She's fine. Look at her."

"Uh, Reka." Tiffany shrunk beside me.

I ignored her and was grateful Peter couldn't poke or kick me under the table. There was anger coursing through my veins.

I smelled the fear coming off Peter and many of the other pack members. My rage was feeding on it.

"YOU ARE NOT LISTENING!" My father leaned forward in his chair. A drop of blood trickled from of one of his balled fists barely suspended over the kitchen table. His eyes were full-blown gold. He was near shifting.

Tiffany sucked in a noisy breath.

Instead of fear, my body trembled with fight, not flight. "I heard every word you said!"

Dad studied my eyes, and as he did, his stare became cool, eyes almost black. "Reka Cassady, as your father and alpha of this pack, I no longer have a place for you in my blood—"

Gasps echoed around the room.

I froze. Anger mixed with fear overwhelmed me as he continued.

"—or in my heart, and, more importantly, in my pack until you come to your senses. Leave my kitchen now, without the human, and you may go in peace until a time when I can look at you without wanting to give you a good shaking."

Dad placed his hands, palms down on the table, and stared at me with cold hard eyes while a rally of adrenaline induced heartbeats flushed my skin.

I knew everyone in the room was holding their breath. My father had just threatened me with death. Anger wound around my spine. I felt my eyes heat up with rage.

Raz stood and moved toward me. "Best to do what he says."

The pack spread, leaving me an opening to the screen door. I looked at Peter. He lowered his eyes but clearly was as freaked out as me.

A sound broke the silence in the room. It was Tiffany. She grabbed my hand as tears ran over her cheeks. "Please don't leave me here. What will my parents say? Will I be safe?" Her eyes implored.

I jumped to my feet and knocked my chair over—it slid across the room—then I hammered a fist on the table. I pointed my finger at my father. "Dakota Cassady, you would separate me from a friend that needs me. You remove me, an alpha as strong and fierce as you, from a pack that needs my strength, as well? For what? Because I demand my rightful place, the ability to prove my strengths and capabilities? Because I refuse to be a mother instead of a leader like you?"

I glared at him through wolf eyes, my heart beating loudly in my ears. "Your anger for me, and a disrespect for this pack makes your decisions irrational and unbeneficial.

I took in a deep breath, then said, "I, Reka Cassady, challenge you for leadership." I pointed at the screen door leading to our back yard. "Today. Right now. Let's take it out back."

Holy Crap! I may have just signed my own death warrant..

Chapter Twenty-Six

<u>CALASTAIR</u>

I felt my muscles tighten as her words soaked in. "My father is...here? Like, in person?"

I wasn't mentally ready to see or talk to him. Conversations with my father were not easy. Many times, I planned what I wanted to say well in advance to try to figure out what his arguments would be. There was also a realization attached to his presents. There were other ways he could talk to me if he wanted. But if he was here in the flesh, that could only mean one thing.

My test had been judged.

"Best not to keep him waiting," Lana said.

I took a couple deep breaths, imagining what I could say. "Did he look mad?" I asked like a toddler concerned it would be punished.

"He looked, well, like your father," she answered. Sympathy seeped into her words as she no doubt sensed my concern. "Sorry, hon. It's hard to tell with him."

I understood. "Thanks, Lana." I shuffled toward the back door.

Lana gave me a reassuring smile as I walked past. It was at that moment a realization sparked in my mind. I thought about how much she had done for me since I came here. About how she took care of all these kids but still found time to help me, even if it was just by giving advice. Even when we disagreed, she had always meant the best for me, even though she was under no obligation to. I never appreciated that till now.

I walked through the kitchen, my feet feeling as if they were trudging through sand. Once in the mud room, I looked out the back door. The yard was cluttered with bright, primary colored plastic toys. Toward the back wooden fence, I saw my dad standing with his back to me. Wavy brown hair fell down to his shoulders, clasped hands rested in the small of his back. With one last deep breath, I opened the door and walked out.

I stepped onto the grass and straightened my back, as he always instructed me to.

"Hello, Father," I said, with words that lacked affection.

He didn't turn around. Instead, he looked over the fence at the neighbor's tree.

"I haven't been on this plane in centuries," he said. "I get so busy with the other dimensions I forget the beauty Earth can produce." A red leaf detached from the tree. It swirled in the gust of wind till my father plucked it from the air. He twirled it as he studied it.

"The whole kingdom is always spinning in a circle. Birth, life, death, and repeat, always changing. So different from the stagnant realm we come from. It's beautiful."

"You find death beautiful?"

He turned and looked at me with eyes as silver as mine. He wore a gray suit and white shirt, which made him look remarkably out of place in the disarray of the backyard.

"It all depends on how you look at things, my son." He placed the leaf gently on the ground. "After all, on this dimension, the death of one being can give life to another. Plants, for example, grow from the decomposition of others. And I do rather enjoy flowers."

I wasn't in the mood for a lesson. "I'm assuming you didn't come all the way here to talk about daffodils."

His expression remained still, neither cold nor warm. "You're right. Let's talk." He gestured to an old picnic table. "Let's sit down."

I watched him take his place at the table. So many times in my life have I heard him say the words "let's sit down," and nothing good has followed them.

I took my place across from him. The table wobbled on uneven ground and I carefully rested my arms on top and tried to avoid splinters from the flaking paint.

"I came here to inform you the angel conclave has met and has reached judgement on your test," he said as if he was an employer at a job interview.

"Wait! How? I haven't even had a chance to help Reka that much."

"That's rather the point, Calastair. You were sent here as a guarding angel for Reka, but so far you've spent most of your time watching over three other humans."

"Because they were in trouble, and I was partly responsible for piquing their interest in Reka's family, so I thought it was my job to fix it."

"Do you really think your discussions with them effected the decisions they made? Do you think if you never met them they wouldn't have gone into those woods?"

I lowered my eyes to my hands. They nervously peeled the flacking paint from the table. "No, I suppose not. But I saw something happening and tried to help. I don't understand why that's a bad thing!"

"There are rules, Calastair."

"Oh, rules, rules, rules." I slapped my palms on the table as I stood. "That's all I hear about. Well, because I broke a rule, I might be able to save the memory of a couple of kids. Tell me that's not worth it!"

My father sighed. "Nevertheless, the conclave has to consider it in their judgment. They decided—"

"I know what they decided." I crossed my arms and turned away. "That I didn't pass their little test. That I wouldn't be allowed back into heaven." There was a pause as the words soaked in. I always knew it was a possibility, but the reality finally set in.

"I'm sorry, son," he said in a low voice.

A cool gust of wind brushed my cheek. I pictured home's golden cities and silver streets. They felt further away now. "Did you agree with them?" I asked.

"Actually, I was your biggest proponent."

The words surprised me. I turned to look at him. "Really?"

He nodded. "The choices you made showed me your character. It took a lot of heart to put your trial aside and help those children. You knew that doing so put yourself at risk, but you did it anyway because you thought it was the right thing to do. Being willing to sacrifice something you hold dear to help others is a mark of a great man. I tried to explain that to the conclave. But they found my argument biased."

I stared at him for a moment. I wasn't used to hearing such flattery.

"I'm surprised to hear that from you. Growing up you were always strict about following the rules. No excuses."

"That's true, and perhaps I was a bit too hard. It might surprise you to hear but I was a bit rebellious myself when I was younger. After all, I did marry your mother, a fae."

The mention of my mother brought heat to my blood. "Then why did you spend most of my life trying to make me fall in line!

Telling me how I should act or what I should do. I'm half fae, but it's like you've been trying to erase Mom's personality from me." I felt moisture pool in the corner of my eye.

It was my father's turn to avert his gaze. "It wasn't that I was trying to erase her." He turned and gazed again at the tree. "You have to understand, your mother...she enjoyed rubbing people the wrong way. Till one day she angered the wrong person and it got her killed. It's those traits that took her from me. I didn't want to lose you, too."

The honesty hit me like a punch to the gut. I had never really considered what Mom's death had been like for my father. I was too young to think of such things. He was always the strong and stern one. I always assumed it hadn't affected him much, but I don't know why I thought that. "So, what now?"

He turned back to me. "Well...procedure would say your powers should be removed and you would stay with Lana till you've finished school."

I shuttered at the thought of losing my powers. It took a long time to get used to having them limited when I arrived here. Having them stripped would be similar to learning to walk again. "There's got to be another option."

I paced between the plastic toys. "You could make me Reka's full-fledged guarding angel."

"Guarding angels are assigned as representatives of heaven. Since you've been banished, the conclave wouldn't allow it, especially with your tendency to involve yourself with others."

He was right. It wouldn't take the conclave long to strip those powers from me. I searched my memory for any angel positions that would allow me to keep my abilities. "I got it! You could make me a Watcher! It's perfect. Watchers are allowed to intervene when something bad is happening but aren't tied to one particular person."

My father eyes darted back and forth as he considered that. "There hasn't been a Watcher in centuries. They tended to overstep their bounds and challenge the conclave. I'm not confident they would allow it."

"But they might!" I grew excited with the thought. "If I don't follow the Watchers' rules, they can take my powers away. If I do, maybe I'll be able to earn my way back home. It'd be like restarting my trial. The best part is I don't even have to keep my identity a secret because Watchers are permitted to reveal themselves."

"Although I would be careful with that," he advised. "Many humans won't react well to finding out who you are."

"So, you're down with it?" I asked hopefully.

He stared at me for a moment. Then I saw his features soften. He walked up and wrapped his arms around me. "I know I don't say it, but I'm proud of you, son."

Before I could respond, I felt lightheaded. The world spun around me. I might have fallen if my father hadn't held me up. A bright light encapsulated me, coursing over my skin in waves that intensified till I could see nothing but the bright light. And in a burst, it was gone. My senses came back to me and I stumbled back as my father released me. He shined a slight smile.

There was a rustling behind me. I turned to see my wings had been returned. The white feathers with red tips were a sight for sore eyes. I stretched them out to their full length. It felt good, like stretching a muscle after a long sleep.

"Now, remember," my father said, "you're still in training. There's a lot of abilities you haven't mastered yet. So be careful."

Suddenly, I wished I had paid more attention during training. It all seemed so boring at the time. If I knew I'd someday end up on Earth maybe I'd have focused more. But knowing me, probably not. It would feel good to be able to tell Reka who I really was. As a supernatural creature herself, the harm of telling her was minimal, and I had always hated keeping it a secret from her.

Then out of the blue, I felt pain. Then again, felt wasn't the right word. It was more a sense of pain. As if I was aware of pain that wasn't actually there. But I still clenched my side. "Whoa, that's weird. Did something get messed up in the power transfer? I feel like something's clamped down on my side."

"It's not you," he said calmly. "You're sensing pain from someone else. Someone you were focused on."

Reka! I tried to focus on her. I reached out with my senses to see where she was, but they were erratic. I saw trees, buildings of Reed City, and streets. I tried to concentrate only on Reka. For a moment there was nothing, then I saw a flurry of claws and gnashing teeth. In the confusion, I got a quick glimpse of her house. "Reka. She's in trouble. I got to help her!"

My father nodded. "Go; do what you have to do."

There was more for us to discuss, more that I had to say, but it would have to wait. I slipped into The Gray and took to the air, carried by my newly acquired wings. I glanced back to see my father vanish in a burst of bright light. I wondered when I'd see him again.

But I tried to put that out of my mind, along with everything else that had happened. Reka was in trouble. That was all that mattered now.

Chapter Twenty-Seven

<u>REKA</u>

Raz and Papo spoke at once, "You can't let her do this, Dakota," Papo said. "Don't be foolish, Reka," Raz warned.

The rest of the pack looked like carefully placed mounts from the taxidermist.

"Reka has not respected my wishes for months," my father said. "Now she belligerently challenges me in front of my pack, and a human. This time her behavior cannot go unaddressed." He turned to face me. "I've given you a chance to walk out that door and cool down. As an alpha, and my daughter, you may still take it. Because I say so. Listen to your inner voice. Do you hear everyone in this room? You won't because I severed that tie with my words, and—"

"And," I shouted, "I further sever our relationship with my words." I pointed to the screen door. "We end this now. As permitted, I want to start as humans and shift at the commend to fight. Papo, I choose you to mediate the challenge." I pointed to Raz. "You will keep the pack off me when I kill him."

Tiffany gasped and jumped from the table. "Kill? As in, one of you murders the other. Right in front of us? I don't do death. I'm going home now."

Bogdan jumped up as Tiffany ran out the back door.

"Bogdan. Wait!" my father shouted. "Peter will go after the girl and take her to Lana. I don't want him here right now, anyway."

Peter turned to me, then Dakota, his alpha. "You are actually going through with this?"

"I gave her a chance; two of them, Peter. As pack leader, I cannot legally ignore this threat. She is living her eighteenth year.

And even though it's not complete, it is within her rights. I must respond. This is the law we live by. Go now, before I think twice about *your* loyalty."

With one last glance at me, Peter ran from the kitchen. There was no fear in me, just anger, as I turned my back on the alpha of the Newaygo pack and walked out of the house and into the backyard.

A circle was formed. All pack members joined hands in solidarity and locked Papo and Raz inside the ring.

"The fight has been challenged from flesh to fur, and so it will be..." As Papo spoke of rules and regulations, I briefly wondered what was going through Peter's mind as he ran after Tiffany. I couldn't feel him anymore. I felt hollow, empty, and briefly wondered if it was the way a woman feels right after childbirth.

The pack bond was really broken. A fire inside me had longed for this day. And now it was here, and I was numb.

I watched my father stand proud and tall with a precision that showed he was okay with this. It was just as well. If I stayed and he remained pack alpha, I would never be all that I wanted to be, and I'd rather be dead than alive as a mate to a wolf and nothing more. Like slicing a razors over my skin, I felt this new pain, but knew if I survived, the afterward would bring clarity and healing. But you will lose your father, a voice softly whispered in my mind.

"Are you both ready?" Paco looked at me, eyes liquid gold, no fear on his face.

"Yes." I nodded at Papo and stole a look at Raz. He stood tall, but there was pain in his furrowed brow and downturned lips.

I moved my gazes away as I heard my father's loud, gruff, voice growl. "Yes."

"When I blow the whistle, the change and fight begins, until it ends with only one reigning alpha and the death of a wolf."

Dad crouched, eyes feral, lips snarling. I was startled for a second but swiftly got into attack mode. I bent at the waist, arms spread, ready to leap.

The whistle sounded. I watched my father fall to his knees as the change began to take him. Surprisingly, he dove at me with an earsplitting growl, snout just beginning to elongate around a human face.

A gut-wrenching blow to my abdomen knocked the wind out of me. I flew backward and up over the heads of the pack until my back smacked the trunk of a black walnut tree outside the circle. My dad was on his knees, moaning, groaning, bones cracking, claws sprouting, face elongating when I fell from the tree trunk and ran towards the pack's unbroken circle. I leapt and howled into a morning breeze. I was a wolf before my paws pounded my father's back, now covered with fur, and drove his body to the ground.

The smell of fear was wild around me. Uncontrollable hunger consumed me. I wrapped my maw around my father's throat and dug deep. Blood trickled onto my tongue, electrified me. With a shake of his head and a twist of his body, my father dislodged my bite and I landed on my back, head bouncing off the ground. Heavy on my chest, my father's huge wolf forehead pushed against mine and angry gold eyes challenged. I could barely breathe with the weight and strength of him. As I tried to take in a breath, I caught a smile on Raz's face and a large set of white wings with red tips heading downward toward us.

Chapter Twenty-Eight

<u>CALASTAIR</u>

I arrived at Reka's house. From above, I saw a circle of wolves in the backyard. They surrounded two others. I felt Reka's essence in one of the wolves in the circle, and her father was the other. As I dove down, I saw Reka pinned under her father's paws, struggling to free herself from his weight. This certainly wasn't some sort of sparring exercise. The animosity given off by the two of them was as thick as the wind I soared through. The circle of wolves paced anxiously, teeth bared and heads down, waiting for a victor to the contest. A victory I worried would leave the other dead.

That wasn't something I could risk. I tucked my wings against my back and swooped down into a near free fall. Once below the tree line, I slid out of The Gray. Gliding a few feet above the wolves I drew a line with my finger that produced a wall of light. It smacked Dakota's side and knocked him off Reka. With both wolves on either side of the wall, I snapped my fingers, causing it to explode. The blast wasn't powerful enough to cause damage; it was just enough to send the two back and away from each other.

I landed in the middle of the wolf circle. "That's enough! This fight is over!" I declared with as much authority as I could muster.

Reka rolled onto her feet, teeth bared, and snarled at me.

"Hey, don't take that tone with me!" I snapped back.

Her eyes darted to my wings. She raised her head and cocked it at me. Under different circumstances, I would have found it amusing.

Feeling my awareness click back on, I noticed the numerous amounts of snapping jaws drawing closer from the circle of wolves.

All eyes drawn on me, the intruder who dared to attack their alpha. "Back off! You think any of you are a threat to an angel? I could take all of you while drinking dew from a mountain!"

It was a bluff of course. With my lack of training, I was fairly confident the pack would overpower me. But they hesitated. Which was all I needed. In a swift motion I spun around, creating another wall of light at the wolf packs feet. Instead of detonating it like last time, I stretched the energy upward and created a dome around Reka, her father, and myself. The action incised the pack on the outside. Behind the light I could see their shadowy figures throwing themselves against the barrier, creating a thud as if they slammed against a wood fence. their muffled howls haunted the air as they clawed at the wall in a desperate attempt to reach their alpha. The barrier wouldn't be able to keep them out for long at this rate.

Dakota rolled back onto his paws; his fiery eyes locked onto me. I expected him to lunge at my throat, but the man was no fool. Seeing my true form, he must have known a frontal attack would be dangerous. Instead he began to prowl, head down and fangs bared, looking for an opportunity to strike.

I kept him in the corner of my eye but faced Reka. "Look, I don't know what brought all this on, but I can take a good guess. You've told me a lot about your struggles to find your place in the pack, and the pressures that it puts on you. But I wanted to tell you something I just learned. There's always more options. It's scary when those options take you off a path you've always known or were expected to travel. But that doesn't mean it's the wrong way to go."

"You see, Reka, you don't have to fight him, because you already have the right to choose your own path. The pack only has as much power over you as you let it. Decide your own path, and whatever you decide, I promise I'll be there beside you."

My attention faltered for a moment, and Dakota took advantage. With the speed of a viper he lunged at me, slamming his forehead into my side. The pain was minimal, but it was enough to knock the wind from me and send me to the ground. I readied for another attack, but to my surprise I turned to see Dakota shifting back into his human form. His bones twisted and cracked as he did so. It was an unpleasant sight to behold, I couldn't imagine how they could stand it.

"I knew there was something different about you, Calastair," Dakota said as his human face formed. "Never would have guessed you were an angel, though." As his spine reset, he straitened to his full imposing height. "But I don't care who you are, you have no right to interfere in pack tradition. And for the record. I never intended to kill my own daughter. Just teach her a lesson. Leave now, or when that barrier of yours falls you'll feel the strength of my pack."

Part of me wanted to stand up to him, but that was the wrong play here. I invaded his territory, attacked and caged him. It was a miracle he was offering to let me leave without a fight at all. I had told Reka what I had come here to say, there wasn't any reason to stay. Giving Dakota a respectful nod, I took flight and dropped the barrier. The pack swarmed around their alpha in a protective stance. I slipped into The Gray and perched on the roof of the house far enough away to evade even werewolf senses, but close enough to witness Reka's decision.

Chapter Twenty-Nine

<u>REKA</u>

My father towered over me in the flesh. A deep threatening rumble in my throat edged for release. I was still the wolf. He hadn't killed me and told Cal he never intended to as if he knew he would win.

I could still do this. My low rumbling growl turned into a whimper. *No. I can't.*

Cal was right. This was wrong. I was lucky my father just wanted to teach me a powerful lesson.

A silence surrounded us as if nature paused in the ebb of a storm. Fall leaves held fearlessly to their misfortune. Others floated to the ground around us, soundlessly.

I let my body twist, creak, and reform as I rose easily under human flesh. Tears rolled down my cheeks as I stood before my father. The pack surrounded us and moved in closer. I raised my arm, raked hair away from my face, and avoided Peter's gaze on the crowd. This was between me and my father.

"You could've killed me, Dad. I might have tried again if not for Calastair." My voice was strong, but the tears gave my true feelings away. "And by change if I had succeeded, it could've destroyed your pack. I'll never get to be the person I want to be... No. *Need* to be under your rules. I can't let myself get out of control again. I'll be eighteen right after graduation. I know I can leave then, but I want to distance myself for a while, starting today. I was wrong to challenge you. I hope you will forgive me some day." I looked deep into Dad's eyes. They were not his alpha eyes, and revealed pain and regret.

"Where will you go?" my father asked.

I caught a twinge of concern in Papo's frown. Adelina put her fingers into her husband's hip pocket, and he patted her hand before moving to my father's side. Raz already stood on the other side of dad. Their eyes showed the respect they had for him, and the way he had handled me today. He really had no intention of killing me. I saw that in his eyes before Calastair arrived and stopped me from making a complete fool of myself.

"I'd *like* to stay at Lana's until I graduate and until I turn eighteen, Dad," I said, and gave my father some long overdue respect by not insisting. I also let the pack know I was still his daughter. "Then as planned, I'll enter EMU in August with Tiffany." I shot Papo and Raz a glance as I added, "Don't worry about me, I *can* take care of myself."

"If this is what you wish," my father said. "I can't stop you from leaving after you're eighteen, anyway. I'll give you the next few weeks to think about that. I'd like to see you before you leave for college, but I won't interfere with your plans over the summer."

I nodded. In most families, now would be the time to hug and make up. But in a wolf pack it's all about strength and respect. I lowered my gaze. "I'm going to go up to the house and pack a few things. Will you call Lana?"

"Yes," my father said. He turned to the others. "We got a late start today. Let's see if we can make up for it."

Some of the men in the pack had jobs in town. The women turned toward the house.

Raz stepped in my direction. "Reka. I'll walk up with you and give you a hand."

I smiled at Raz. "Thanks."

"I just called Johnathan," Peter said as he walked up beside me. I didn't even realize he'd moved away. "He's on his way over to pick us up."

"Us?" I felt a wave of thankfulness and held back tears.

"Wherever you go, I'm going." He raised a hand and thwarted my half-baked attempt at a rebuttal. "Don't argue with me," Peter said and then spoke to my father. "I'll be at collage with her, anyway. Together, we'll be fine. The pack will never be far away. I can come back if you need me. Let me have this."

My father's eyes were heavy on mine. Finally, he nodded Peter his acceptance. I mentally felt pack tension drop dramatically and took a deep breath. They may have scattered but I could feel them again. I swallowed the lump in my throat.

"Do you mind calling Lana?" I asked Dad, though it was not necessary since he'd already said he would. I wanted to hold on to the feeling I had right then. It felt good. "You don't have to."

"I'll contact her," Dad said. "Go pack."

The air was crisp and fragrant with the smell of dried grass and decaying leaves. It was a good smell. Earthy. One season ending, Earth making room for the birth of spring. I listened to the crackle of cold ground under foot and felt the promise of many adventures in the coming year.

As we cleared the wood line, I spotted Cal on the top of our roof, his beautiful wings tucked behind him. I smiled and the look on my face and feeling in my heart displayed my gratitude. I pointed up at him. "My guardian angel." I said.

Peter tightened his grip on my hand. Raz glanced up with a grin, but quietly walked across the field beside me and up the porch steps. When I passed through the front door, I knew deep inside it would be the last time I entered without a phone call or an invitation. It hurt, felt scary, but it also made my chest swell.

Raz turned toward the kitchen as Peter and I headed up the stairs.

I watched him until he disappeared. "Are you mad at me?" I asked Peter as we walked down the upstairs hallway.

Peter stopped in front of my bedroom door. His face was hard, lips tight, brow furrowed. "Damn, Reka. You almost ripped your father's throat out. And if it wasn't for Cal and your father's strength you might've been dead right now."

"I know! And can we drop it and move on?" I asked, anger swelling in my chest. "We're animals, Peter. When will you get that? It's about strength. That's why I'll never understand the inability to treat members based on gender."

"Oh, I get that," Peter said. "And so did your father. He let you choose fur because he knew you had the advantage. Your choice to use it, is probably what put that respect in his eyes. Didn't you get that? In a split second, you went from his pup to a formable equal. He won't challenge you again." Peter lowered his head. "You got what you wanted. Your dad may second think his archaic rules."

I thought about that as I opened my bedroom door. Rite of passage I supposed. While I felt the chains of childhood and gender control fall from my neck, I felt a weight on my shoulders. I was on my own. Not that the pack wouldn't be there if I needed them. I was still family. I felt it. I could feel them.

"I don't for one minute think my father put his life on the line to test me," I said, but boy, what that wasn't true." *Crap.* At that moment, I was very happy to have my winged friend.

"Come on, Reka, don't be an idiot. Own up to it," Peter said as he pushed by o get into the bedroom.

I whipped around in front of him and pointed a finger.

Peter grabbed my finger and held it tight. "The fact that he didn't confront us about handling Tiffany and the stray wolf attack says it all. You got what you wished for. Respect. Don't wallow in it. Wear it proudly."

"Maybe so," I said with a smile.

"I think you both handled everything well," Cal said as he stepped out of The Gray.

I yelped.

"Jeez, you scared the crap out of me!" I felt the hairs on my neck bristle. "Can't you knock on a door or window or something like most people?"

Cal grinned. "I'm not most 'people,'" he said with finger quotes and a chuckle. "This is going to work out well."

"Which part?" Peter asked.

"Us," Cal said, then stared at me, a question resting behind his lips.

"What?" I asked.

Instead of answering, Cal turned to Peter.

"I didn't ask her," Peter said, hands raised palms facing the angel.

"Do I look like a picture hanging on a wall?" I bumped my chest with my thumb. "I'm standing right here. What's up?"

Peter pulled his eyes off Cal's and turned to me. "Cal asked about... he wanted to know..."

"Okay," I said and turned away, "If neither of you wants to respond, just head downstairs and wait for me to pack."

"I asked Peter about you cutting yourself." Cal swayed from one foot to the other.

I smiled before I turned around. "I haven't cut myself since you pushed yourself into my life, angel-boy."

"I'm far from a boy," Cal said.

"Hey, at least it's no longer alien-boy," Peter said.

"This is true," I said. "So, let's change the subject because we are not going to discuss my previous frame of mind."

"I'll give you that," Cal said. "However, if you start again..."

"I won't!"

Cal was silent for a heartbeat. "I have a plan for us, but I don't want to discuss it without Johnathan and Tiffany because it includes them."

"Okay," I agreed and wondered why he even brought it up. "But just so we're all on the same page, let's get something straight. If your plan has anything to do with a pack of our own, you thinking because you are an angel with all kinds of magic powers does not give you the right to be the boss of me."

Cal reared his head back and laughed. "Maybe not," he said. "However, the four of you will head off to another part of the state in just a few months, and the ability to keep in contact with your pack, or in Tiffany and Johnathan's case, parents, happens to be the perfect setting for what I have in mind because I'm going with you."

"Okay then. So, what would that perfect situation involve?" Peter asked.

"All in good time," Cal answered, and sauntered away. In seconds, he was gone. "All in good time," the echo of his voice shared his humor.

"How's the packing coming?" Raz shouted from the first floor and I jumped three inches. I frowned at where Cal had disappeared, and shouted at Raz, "Just getting started."

"Can you come down for a second?" Raz called back. "Your friend Johnathan is here with a surprise."

I ran down the stairs, Peter at my heels, and when we stepped through the front door I gasped.

Johnathan waved from the window of a black, four door, Jeep Wrangler, all shiny and new.

"Is that yours?" I asked, but from the grin on his face I knew the answer.

"Yep. Thanks to Grandpa," Johnathan answered.

I screeched, hands clapping, and bounced down the porch stairs way too excited. "I can drive it, too!"

"So not going to happen, man," Johnathan shouted from the Jeep. "But dudes, we have wheels at EMU. I can drive us there."

"Wow." I giggled and climbed into the passenger seat. "I can't believe your parents let your grandfather buy you a new Jeep for your first vehicle."

"Yeah," Peter said. "A beater maybe, but man, this is worth some bucks."

"Right?" Johnathan said. "Grandpa talked Mom into it. Dad wasn't too happy, but Grandpa said he wants to see me enjoy my inheritance while he still can. Cool dude, my grandad."

"I guess so," I said while Peter leaned over the console from the back seat to play with the GPS unit in the dash.

"Yeah, man. And good old Dad and Mom said they'd pay for gas and insurance as long as I stay in school."

"Sounds like a good bribe to me," I laughed, and stuck my tongue out at Papo and Raz. They burst into laughter.

I heard Cal whisper, *"Perfect"*, and glanced around but saw nothing. I frowned.

The alien angel had definitely winged his way into my life. However, he seemed way too happy for the happenings of the day. But then he *had* saved my butt, and my father's pride.

"*And you tossed the razors,*" Cal whispered.

"Does anyone else hear Cal's laughter," I asked.

Johnathan and Peter frowned at me.

Maybe I'm imagining it.

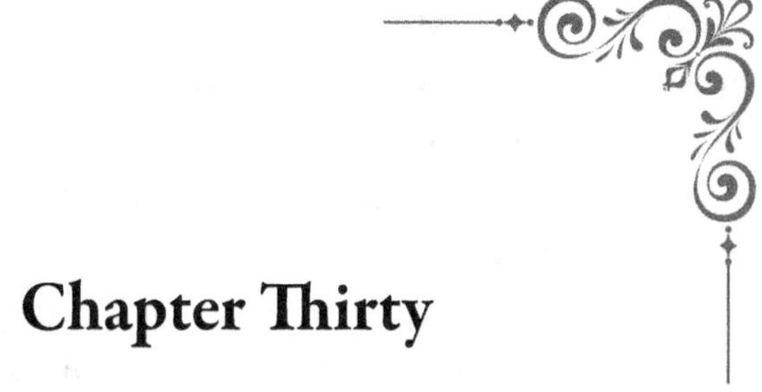

Chapter Thirty

CALASTIER

I couldn't help but smile. The day could have ended horribly, but Reka and her father managed to avoid bloodshed, at least, for the most part. Pride swelled within me knowing I was partly responsible for the events ending the way they did. It was a feeling unfamiliar to me. Perhaps it was what all angels felt when they helped people through their hard times. It was an intoxicating feeling.

The Jeep sped away, leaving a dusty trail swirling in the wind. I watched it from the rooftop, hidden within The Gray. Reka's pack shuffled around the front yard. Her father watched the car disappear around the bend into the trees. I still didn't like the man. I could be holding a grudge from being manhandled earlier, but it was his controlling personality that gave me the most pause. However, looking at him now, I could sense a vulnerability behind his rigid exterior. Even if others couldn't see it, I knew it hurt him to see Reka go. For his faults, there was no denying the pressure the man was under. Being responsible for the pack, a member of the council, and raising a rebellious daughter was a lot to juggle. Perhaps he would find Reka's leaving to be beneficial for himself as well.

Expanding my wings, I took to the air with a couple powerful thrusts. The woods seemed so peaceful from above. Deer bobbed and weaved through the trees; squirrels chased each other across branches. A few hawks glided nearby, searching for their next meal. For the first time, I felt the freedom they did. My test was over, and even though I failed to reenter heaven's gates, I managed to help Reka through a difficult decision. And I hoped somewhere, my father was watching the events with a grin.

The Jeep appeared in front of me, tucked between the lines of trees. I swooped and gently touched down on top of its roof. The radio blared within. A strong, fast-paced beat pulsated through the truck's frame. I could hear Reka, Johnathan, and Peter's voices shouting over the music. Though the music was too loud to make out what was said, the laughter that rang told me they were all happy.

They probably felt freedom for the first time, just as I did. It took a lot of guts for Peter to leave the pack and set out with Reka, blazing an unknown trail. I admired him for that, though it would probably be a long time till I'd admit that to his face.

In the meantime, I remained in The Gray and let the two enjoy the moment. There was much more to do before they were out of danger. There was still a wolf somewhere close by, searching for Tiffany. It was hard to say how he would react if they found out she was sheltered at Reka's old home for the moment. There could still be violence between the packs. Not to mention the council was still looking to wipe Tiffany and Johnathan's minds. Lana could keep them at bay for a while. But it was a terrible position to put her in. A fact she would, no doubt, remind me of.

Hiding from the council would be hard, if not impossible. I may be able to shield them from most of the members, but I doubted my untrained powers could match the jinn's. There was a chance evading them long enough would make them think it wasn't worth the trouble. But it was more likely they would view it as a challenge to their control and bring their full fury down on us.

The guitar solo kicked in and made the windows of the Jeep rattle. Yeah, I'd let them enjoy their newfound freedom for now. Soon, we would talk about our next step. And if hiding wasn't the viable option, then finding a safe place to stay was the way to go. But it had to be a place where they could live free without prosecution. Somewhere that had rules to keep nonhuman entities safe from humans and each other. Somewhere they could essentially hide in plain sight.

I just didn't know how they would react when I told them we allz might have to go Down Under.